The Discarded Daughter Book 3 – Reunited

A Pride & Prejudice Variation

By Shana Granderson, A Lady

The characters and events portrayed in this book are fictitious. Any similarity to real persons, living or dead, is coincidental and not intended by the author. Some historical figure's names are used in the story but none of the situations that they are portrayed in are real.

Cover Art Design by:

Veronica Martinez Medellin

ISBN 13: 978-0-473-56888-7

CONTENTS

DEDICATION

This book, like all that I write, is dedicated to the love of life, the holder of my heart. You are my one and only and you complete me. You make it all worthwhile and my world revolves around you.

ACKNOWLEDGEMENT & THANK YOU

First and foremost, thank you E.C.S. for standing by me while I dedicate many hours to my craft. You are my shining light and my one and only.

I want to thank my Alpha, Will Jamison and my Betas Caroline Piediscalzi Lippert, and Kimbelle Pease. A special thank you to Kimbelle who had been a great help and has dedicated much time and effort to making this book better. To both Gayle Surrette and Carol for taking on the role of proof-reader and final editing, a very big thank you to you. All of you who have assisted me please know that your assistance is most appreciated.

Thank you to Veronica Martinez Medellin who created the cover art.

My undying love and appreciation to Jane Austen for her incredible literary masterpieces is more than can be expressed adequately here. I also thank all of the JAFF readers who make writing these stories a pleasure.

INTRODUCTION

This is book 3 in a 4-book series.

The Bennets have just discovered their kidnapped daughter and sister. Bennet cannot believe that she is the one that he has been corresponding with, and losing to, in chess by post for almost two years. How will the families move forward? Will Thomas Bennet assert his rights as Elizabeth's father and demand that she re-joins her Bennet family? What of the Fitzwilliams? Would Lady Elaine be able to endure the loss of her much-loved daughter after the loss of her beloved Reggie? If she is to return to the Bennets how will that influence the growing romance between Elizabeth and William? Many of the above questions are answered in the opening chapters dear readers so you will not be left in suspense for long.

We follow the families as they learn to live with a new reality. We see the reaction of the Ton to the news as well as the villain's vociferous reactions when they find out that all of their prior assumptions about Elizabeth have been wrong. Mrs. Fitzpatrick (the former Lady Catherine) eventually manages to get one of her men employed at Pemberley.

We are privy to her plans for her ultimate revenge of her former family and at the same time we see what George Wickham has planned and how he intends to double cross his employer after enduring years of abuse at her hands. A new challenge rears its ugly head with an eye on our heroine and making her his by any means before Elizabeth is out at the age of sixteen and we find out how and if he is dealt with.

Book 3 ends at the start of the confrontation between the

forces of good and evil. You will know the result of the confrontation in the first chapter of the final book in the series. Book 4 is complete and being edited now. It will be published in June 2021.

CHAPTER 1

She could not understand it, but Elizabeth felt relief and comfort and hugged the woman in closer for a moment, unable to reject such pure emotion as she saw on her face before this woman hugged her. After a long moment of silence, while all those around them stared, everyone seemed to find their voices at once and began talking over one another.

"Perhaps we should pay attention to the rest of our party for a moment, Miss Bennet." Lizzy teased her. Jane's laugh barely hid a sob of relief as she reluctantly acquiesced. They mutually broke the hug, Jane's smile watery, when Lizzy instead took her hand and squeezed it gently in appreciation.

"**Does someone want to enlighten me as to just what is going on**?" Lizzy raised her voice in an attempt to get everyone to at least focus, unable to quite check her smile when she heard Miss Bennet's soft laugh.

Bennet was still staring at her as if he were in a dream, feeling like none of this was real. Elaine knew; she had not a shred of a doubt that Lizzy's birth family was the Bennets.

"Excuse me for asking you this, Lady Elizabeth," Jane ventured, "but are you the natural daughter of the Dowager Countess of Matlock?"

"No, Lizzy is not my natural daughter but is truly my daughter in every way that counts. It has never been a secret that Lizzy was a foundling that we adopted," Elaine stated gently.

Bennet found his voice. "When and where was she found? Also, Lady Elizabeth, would you object if I viewed your cross?" he asked, not wanting to frighten the young lady that he now was on the verge of believing was his daughter. Elizabeth looked to her mother and Andrew, and both nodded yes. She removed the cross and handed it to Mr Bennet, watching him closely, and saw that it had the most extraordinary effect on him. He fell into the nearest chair weeping like he had not wept in many years as he held his mother's cross in his hands, the very one that Lizzy had been wearing the day that the deranged woman stole her away from him. Tammy and Jane kneeled by him, while his other children looked on in confusion.

"My brother Richard," Andrew pointed to Richard, "and I recovered Lizzy in Sherwood Forest on the twentieth of June 1782. The same man that murdered our father had discarded her." While Andrew was speaking, Richard stuck his head out of the drawing-room and told the butler to have someone summon the Darcys urgently. "My late father put notices in papers and towns in all of the surrounding shires, even some further afield. There was never a response, so my parents adopted Lizzy and recognised her as their daughter just months after she came to live with us."

"It was June when our daughter was kidnapped," Tammy Bennet added while she comforted her husband.

"Good Lord!" Maddie Gardiner exclaimed. "I had just departed Lambton; I assume that the late Earl placed a notice there."

"He did not," George Darcy said as he entered the drawing-room, his family in tow. "I did, and every town that we reached." He looked at Bennet. "We met at Bennington Fields when I purchased the mare for my daughter here." He met Bennet's stare, none getting in the way as Georgiana made a beeline for Elizabeth. "I believe you met William when he visited the Bingleys one Easter." Bennet nodded. "My wife, Lady Anne Darcy, and that young lady," he pointed to his daughter now tucked under Elizabeth's arm, "is my daughter, Georgiana, and the young man behind his mother is my son Alex."

"So, it was the madwoman's paramour who took Lizzy away from us. All the clues he left pointed to the south and a departure from the country. Why did he murder the late Earl?" Bennet was trying to assemble the pieces of information he had been craving for over a decade.

As everyone calmed down, Elizabeth sat on a settee with Georgiana on one side and her mother and Anne de Bourgh on the other. Andrew and Marie sat in chairs right next to Georgiana, while Richard and William stood behind Elaine. Elizabeth was thus surrounded by the family that she knew.

Bennet started the recitation with information about the madwoman and her belief that Lizzy was the [redacted] because she was a girl and not a boy, including the steps that he took to protect his daughter. He moved to that horrendous night when his world came to a standstill, the night his Lizzy had been taken. His wife filled in information about how she and the nursemaid watched over Lizzy to protect her from the deranged woman were drugged.

The story of how they searched for months on end without result was told, and then the unpleasant part of how the deranged woman on her deathbed tried to hurt him by telling him that his precious [redacted] daughter was dead at her hands; as proof, she offered the box that contained a heart. He told of the relief that he felt when the doctor had told him it was a deer's heart, not a human one. Although he knew not where his Lizzy was, he had always felt that she was well.

He finished his part with how, in June of 1789, he had a horrendous feeling that Lizzy was in trouble. Jane then told them about her dreams, and as she was about to tell them what she heard in her dreams, Elizabeth and William both said: "Help me 'aney, help me." All the women were crying, as were most of the men without shame, for this was one of their greatest hopes and their greatest fears culminating before them all. It amazed them all that Elizabeth had had some sort of inexplicable connection with her birth family for the whole of her life. It was also the first time that Elizabeth had no doubt who the Bennets were.

Before they continued, the butler was asked to have some maids take the younger Darcy, Gardiner, and Bennet children to the nursery, all of whom left under protest.

Richard started with who he had seen, now known to be Hodges, discarding Lizzy from the carriage and whipping his horse into a frenzy to leave the area as soon as he saw the Fitzwilliam carriage approach.

Andrew continued with how Lizzy looked similar to the sister they had lost to tragedy, adding how that had in no way influenced their decision to take her home to their parents. The more that the Fitzwilliams talked, and when Elaine added that Lizzy had been like a breath of fresh air that breathed the life back into Snowhaven, the more Bennet understood just how fortunate his daughter had been to be discovered by such good people.

He knew that his Lizzy was intelligent, but he had no idea it was to the degree that he heard the Fitzwilliams describe. The queen routinely requested that Lizzy play and sing for her, and she had perfect recall after reading something but once!

When they reached the part about George Wickham and his attempted murder, that man made yet more and very powerful enemies. A few hours later, they reached the part of the story about Hodges and his group of criminal cronies. Bennet knew without a shadow of a doubt that had someone pointed a weapon at his wife and children, he would have done the same thing that the Earl, a hero in his eyes, had done.

"I just remembered something," Bennet added after the telling was complete. "About two years ago, possibly less, I received a note from someone demanding ten thousand pounds for information about where Lizzy was. There had been so many that had tried to prey on my grief for their personal gain that I consigned it to the fire. I was to write to the Wild Bull Inn in Packwood. If I had, then maybe the late Earl would be alive," Bennet lamented.

"You have a trait in common with Lizzy," Elaine responded. "She, too, likes to take guilt on her shoulders that does not belong to her." Bennet looked questioningly at his second daughter.

"After Papa was shot, I blamed myself. I thought that my being a Fitzwilliam had caused everything bad that had happened. Mama, Aunt Anne, Uncle George, my brothers, and Will all helped me see that there was nothing I did or could do that would have changed who the bad people were. I think Mama is trying to tell you the same thing, Mr Bennet." She paused, looked at her mother and then back at Mr Bennet. "What do I call you? I had a Papa, so neither that nor Father sounds right to me at this time."

"Lizzy," Andrew said, "You are the common bond that makes us all family. The Bennets are your family, so they are our family. What do you think, Mr Bennet and Lizzy, if you address your birth father as Uncle..." Andrew did not remember the man's familiar name in all the confusion of Lizzy's birth family recognising her.

"Thomas. Uncle Thomas will work. I never expected to see my girl again in my lifetime, so she could address me as she pleases and it will be music to my ears."

"I like that, Uncle Thomas." She looked at Tammy Bennet, "That would make you Aunt Tammy?" she asked and Tammy nodded happily.

"You are not going to leave us, are you Lizzy?" Georgiana verbalized the fear that had been building in her since the revelations had begun.

"No, Gigi, I am not. I will *always* be your cousin, that I can promise you," Elizabeth assured her young cousin, glancing around to make sure all knew she was not to be gainsaid in this promise, and her eyes stilled when she saw Perry and Miss Bennet together. "Wait a minute," Elizabeth watched them, noticing how Perry stayed close to her and how solicitous he was being. "Perry, is there some news that you mayhap need to share with the rest of us?"

"It is not the time yet, Lady Eliz..." Jane was cut off by her younger sister.

"My name is Elizabeth and family and friends address me as Lizzy, 'aney!" she used the last name by which she had addressed Jane Bennet. As usual, Elizabeth helped to lighten the mood.

"Alright, *Lizzy*, our news can keep until the morrow," Jane tried to insist, her smile at hearing her name said by her sister truly beautiful to behold.

"Fiddlesticks, Jane! If ever there was a day when good news was welcome, it would be today. It is not every day that one is reunited with one's birth family after so many years. I can guess what yours and my brother-in-law's news is, but mayhap one of you wants to tell us before I guess out *loud*," she teased them.

"Has she always been so impertinent?" Bennet asked of no one in particular.

"Worse!" Richard interjected with a grin.

"Itch, I would mind what I say if you do not want your secrets revealed," Elizabeth threatened playfully.

"Itch?" Perry asked.

"When Lizzy first came to us," Elaine explained, "she could not say Richard, or Rich, so he became Itch, and it has stuck over the years. Is that not so, my Itch?"

"Yes, Mother," Richard replied, with a 'just you wait' look directed at his younger sister.

"Like she called me 'aney instead of Jane or Janey," Jane added.

"There was one name she remembered fully; is there a John in your family?" Richard asked.

"I am John, John Manning," John came forward. Tammy explained how he was her son from her first marriage, who had been accepted as her husband's son in every way that matters, and why she chose that he kept his birth father's last name.

"John and Lizzy used to have their little beds next to each other, and they used to love to play together," Tammy added. "Talking about sons, William," she called her oldest son forward, "was my husband's sister's boy, and when he was orphaned, we adopted him. He is eighteen and at the School of Divinity at Cambridge. James here," she pointed to the boy standing near his father, "is twelve and will start at Eton next year. He was the first child that Thomas and I were gifted after we married. The twins, Kitty and Tom, are in the nursery."

"Kitty?" Anne Darcy asked?

"Her full name is Catherine," Tammy explained.

"Kitty is good," Andrew and Richard said together.

"Wait, Mrs. Bennet, your first name is Tammy correct," Elaine asked, remembering another name Lizzy had uttered when she arrived at Snowhaven.

"'ammy!" Richard and Andrew said as one.

"She mentioned my name as well?" Tammy Bennet was gratified that she had made an impression on her charge at the time.

Elizabeth looked at Perry expectantly, "The floor is yours, Perry."

"Well, per a demand from my impertinent sister-in-law, it is my great pleasure to let you all know that I requested Jane's hand in marriage today, and she did me the great honour of accepting me," Perry announced proudly as he looked at his betrothed lovingly.

"When I think of all the times that we came close to meeting Lizzy over the years, and not asking questions that we should have," Tammy Bennet mused.

"I believe that things happen for a reason," Lady Rose opined. "It was the right time. With my Perry marrying Jane, it was inevitable that Lizzy would meet her birth family, and one way or another they were destined to be sisters again."

"You see Thomas, if you liked the town more you would have heard that the Fitzwilliams had adopted a girl that they recovered in Sherwood, and that would have led you to make inquiries," Tammy surmised.

"One thing that I have learnt, Aunt Tammy, is that we can 'what if' until the end of days, but it will not change anything. All we can do is move forward now," Elizabeth said philosophically.

"Wise girl, that one," Uncle George said with a grin, and his statement earned him a round of laughter.

"I apologize if I am the one who interjects some reality into our reunion, but what are we going to announce and when?" Andrew asked.

"Nothing to apologize for, my Lord;" Bennet responded, "that is a very salient question."

"Can we please dispense with titles, as Lizzy correctly pointed out, we are all family here *Uncle Thomas*. Sorry, Uncle George, you are no longer our only uncle," Andrew grinned.

"Very well Andrew, then back to my question," Bennet said.

"What I suggest," George said, "is that we announce we have discovered a connection to the Bennets of Longbourn, and we are recognising them as an uncle, aunt and cousins." Then he added, "While not revealing the whole truth, there will be nothing announced that is a lie. With those who are not in this room now, and we trust implicitly, we can share the full story, but in my opinion that will allow the families to become well acquainted with one another and make decisions about the way forward."

"Uncle Thomas and Aunt Tammy, you will not force me to leave my Fitzwilliam family, will you?" Lizzy asked with concern.

"No Lizzy, we will never force you or even ask you to do that. Being stripped from your family once in a lifetime is already once too many, so we would never put you or your family through that again," Thomas assured his daughter. "Just having you back in our lives is so much more than I ever dreamed of. As long as we are part of your life in some small way as we all walk this new path together; we will be satisfied." Everyone in the drawing room that loved Lizzy was happy and to see her visibly relax with the assurance that her birth father provided her.

'I will not be losing the family I love and who love me,' Elizabeth exhaled in relief, hugging Gigi tightly as her cousin sobbed with relief. *'Instead, I will be gaining more relatives to love.'*

"Oh, Uncle Thomas," Lizzy cocked her one eyebrow. "There is the little matter of a game of chess, is there not?" She asked playfully.

"That will be a game at which I want to be to be a spectator," George Darcy surmised. "I have looked up your record at Cambridge, Bennet. Will and I are not the only ones in this room who were unbeaten at our alma mater."

"And who has the distinction of being beaten by a certain, impertinent miss," William added.

"Well, there is that," Bennet said.

"I think that, given the emotions of today, we should take a break. What say you that we all meet at Gardiner House on the morrow, so we can continue to get to know one another? We will make sure that Lizzy has the five minutes that it will take her to wipe the board with Bennet," Gardiner ribbed.

"I resent that," Bennet chuckled, "if anyone wants to wager, I say that I will last at least ten minutes!" For the first time since Jane's exclamation some hours ago, there was laughter in the room that contained the newly reunited, now expanded family.

"I would like to extend an invitation to dinner. I do not know about the rest of you, but I am just a little hungry. What say you, Marie, would the cook revolt if we add *one or two* for dinner?" Before Marie could answer, Lady Anne Darcy had a suggestion.

"The cook at Darcy House always prepares far too much. What if we have the footmen bring over the food prepared at our house, Marie? I am sure between our two cooks there will be more than enough, and a good variety of dishes served." Marie agreed, and a message was dispatched to the Darcy's cook while Marie went to smooth any ruffled feathers in her kitchen.

Anne Darcy, Tammy Bennet, Elaine Fitzwilliam, and Maddie Gardiner ascended to the nursery with Elizabeth in tow. Other than baby May, they had the children sit on the floor, so they could explain as easily as possible the changes to the family. When they were done, Tom stood. "So, Lizzy is my sister, but she is my cousin now?" he asked.

"That is correct, Tom," Tammy confirmed.

"Alex is our cousin as well?" Tom asked hopefully.

"Yes, he is," Anne replied.

"Good," Tom smiled, "I like him."

That is all it took, with the added verbal expectation that no one was to discuss anything about the situation with anyone outside of their immediate family. With agreement from the five, the ladies descended to re-join the rest of the family.

When they returned to the drawing-room, Marie let them know that her cook had agreed to the plan for dinner, not without some grumbling about food from another kitchen being served at *her* table.

Andrew and Marie asked the housekeeper and butler to meet them in the study while the table was being set and dinner prepared to be served. They explained their expectation of absolute discretion from the servants, authorised a bonus as an incentive, but made it clear that any gossip traced back to their servants would lead to summary dismissal with no character.

If dinner was a harbinger of the future, then there would be much joy in the extended family. It was louder than normal with so many conversations being held. No formal seating was used nor precedence followed, so each one sat where they desired. Elizabeth had Jane on one side, Anne de Bourg next to Jane, and William on the other with Georgiana next to William. Richard, Perry, John, and William Bennet sat opposite. It was decided with two Williams in the family that William Darcy would be called Will, as many already called him, and the Bennet namesake would remain William. Knowing how much his cousin disliked his given name as a first name, Richard suggested that he be called Fitzwilliam, a suggestion that was roundly rejected by all parties to the discussion.

Bennet was sitting next to George Darcy on one side and Edward Gardiner on the other, across from Andrew and Marie, with Tammy, Anne Darcy, and Lady Rose seated next to one another and Elaine and Maddie opposite them. Bennet mentioned how happy he was with the library that he had expanded significantly when Longbourn was essentially rebuilt. Gardiner had seen the library at Snowhaven, the one time he had been at the house to appraise some items as a favour to the late Earl.

"If I remember, Bennet, and correct me if I err, Andrew, the library at Snowhaven is very large. I would estimate twice yours at Longbourn," Gardiner ribbed his brother-in-law, knowing how much of a bibliophile he was.

"I do not know how large your library is, Uncle Thomas, but I must agree with Uncle Edward, our library is the size of an oversized ballroom," Andrew informed Bennet, who was thinking about how often he would need to visit Lizzy. George Darcy had remained silent with a smirk on his face, waiting until Bennet was well and truly drooling while thinking about his new nephew's library.

"I agree, Snowhaven's library is rather impressive," George Darcy drawled, "except when compared to that at Pemberley." He waited, and chuckled when he saw Bennet's eyes widen in hope.

"Are you trying to tell me, Darcy, that your library is larger than Andrew's?" Bennet was flabbergasted.

"Only three to four times!" George delivered the *coup-de-grâce*.

"I cannot imagine so many tomes!" Bennet was in heavenly shock as he imagined the treasures that would be found in such a library.

"Can I assume that you will want to visit Pemberley when you visit Snowhaven?" Darcy smirked at Andrew when all Bennet could do was nod.

As all good things do, the evening came to an end with plans to meet at Gardiner House on the morrow when an announcement for the times would be drafted and the long-awaited face-to-face chess game played.

Jane had no qualms about her and Perry's announcement being overshadowed when the paper was read by one and all. One, she preferred to share her joy with those she loved, and for the news that one of her greatest prayers had been answered, that their Lizzy had been found? That was worth all the overshadowing in the known world.

Before they departed, Bennet approached his second daughter. "Lizzy, I did not want to overwhelm you, but would you allow me to hug you for the first time in over fifteen years?" he requested with moisture in his eyes. Elizabeth simply nodded and walked forward into her birth father's embrace. It just felt right to both of them and for Bennet, it was the fulfilment of a wish that he never thought would be granted in his lifetime.

CHAPTER 2

After the younger children were in their beds for the night, the adults and the older children sat in the family sitting room at Gardiner House still trying to assimilate everything that had transpired on this most momentous of days.

Looking at her oldest daughter with concern, Tammy said, "Jane, I am sorry that so much attention was taken from yours and Perry's news."

"I was thinking about that at Matlock House when *Lizzy* requested we make the announcement, Mama, and I have no regrets. Today was a miracle. When I saw how Papa was staring at that portrait, I knew, and when Lizzy entered the room wearing Grandmother Beth's cross, all doubts I had were swept away. I would have my news overshadowed today with us being reunited with my sister no matter the day," Jane exhaled slowly to keep her emotions in check as the joy and heartbreak of so many missed chances could be overwhelming if considered closely.

"Father, now that you have found Lizzy, how come she will not live with us?" James asked carefully.

"That is a good question, son," Bennet nodded. His thoughtful and studious son always had the most carefully considered questions which, as this one did, had many levels to both it and the answer. "Let me explain it thusly James. Imagine, son, that tomorrow you met a man or woman who said they were your birth parent. How would you feel at the prospect of leaving the only family that you knew, that loved you, that you came to by no fault of your own or theirs?"

James contemplated his father's hypothetical question. "I would feel like someone was trying to rend me from the only family that I knew and loved, I suppose," James replied slowly, as the longer he considered it the more he internally rebelled at the thought.

"This is the exact reason that I can never demand that Lizzy come live with us. She has a family, one that by the grace of God rescued her after the demented woman's paramour discarded her in the forest. He did not kill her as he was asked to do, but if Lizzy's brothers had not discovered and rescued her, he would have killed her, even if not by his own hand," Bennet explained. "As I said, I could never cause Lizzy the trauma of being torn from the family that loves her. Instead, I suggest we consider it a blessing that they told her she was found and not their natural child and loved her the more for it, so today was not rife with anguish and sorrow while we would naturally feel such happiness as we never thought to have."

"I am beginning to see that it is not as easy as I had hoped, Father," James nodded slowly. "I think I will thank the family of our sister when I get the opportunity. You are right, today could have been much harder."

"It amazed me that Lizzy remembered my name," John offered to the conversation, "I hardly remembered her at all."

"That is expected, John, as you are but three months older than Lizzy," his mother told him.

"We are considered cousins of hers, correct Mother?" William asked.

"For now, at least." Bennet nodded in agreement with his wife. "At some point in the future, *if* all are in agreement, then the true relationship will be revealed."

"We need to send an express to Frank and Hattie," Gardiner turned to the business of matters of the closest concern. "Hattie always felt guilty that she could not do something about her sister. She, in particular, will be overjoyed to know, then eventually see for herself, that Lizzy is well and happy."

"I will write the express if you are willing to send one of your couriers at first light," Bennet agreed and Gardiner nodded as it was too late to send one that evening. He had no doubt that Bennet intended to write the missive before he went to bed so that the courier could depart in the morning with no delay.

"Do you remember when we met Lizzy about ten years distant at the warehouse, Aunt Maddie?" Jane asked.

"My goodness, yes, I do remember now. You said that you felt you knew her and we dismissed it as impossible!" Maddie stared at Jane in all wonder one would have when such seemingly impossible things are proven.

"We came close to her several times over the years," Bennet sighed with longing for the time lost with his daughter. "I have been playing chess with, and of late being routinely beaten by, my daughter for nigh on two years without knowing it! I do not believe that was a coincidence; somehow we were fated to meet again, and serendipity brought us all together in one place today."

"Thomas, you do know what this means, do you not?" Tammy asked with a smile.

"What is that, my love?" Bennet could not fathom what she was hinting at.

"Your days of eschewing the Town are well and truly over!" Tammy laughed at the look of horror on her husband's face.

"Your wife has the right of it, brother. Do you not think that the time has come for you to look at acquiring a townhouse?" Gardiner pointed out.

"You know Papa, if you are interested in purchasing one, Perry mentioned that his mother was thinking of selling the townhouse on Grosvenor square she inherited from her mother as she has not used it in some years, and it just sits empty with a skeleton staff. It is but three houses away from Matlock House," Jane revealed to her family.

"Please ask your betrothed, Jane," Bennet sighed with resignation. "If it is for sale, may we view the house at his convenience?"

"That will be my pleasure, Papa," Jane kissed her father's cheek as she headed to her chamber to dream about the man that she loved.

~~~~~~~/~~~~~~~

After the rest of the guests left, the Fitzwilliams and Darcys were silent for a minute or two when Elizabeth then looked at each of her family members in turn: "Did that truly happen? Did I find my birth family, or, rather, they found me after almost fifteen years? I have so many questions! I forgot to ask what my actual birthday is!" Elizabeth was babbling, rare for her to do, but understandable given the magnitude of the day.

"I asked Tammy Bennet," Elaine offered calmly.

"Do not make me wait, Mama, when was I born?" Elizabeth asked excitedly.

"In 1781, on the fifth day of March," Elaine revealed.

"Lizzy, we share a birthday!" Georgiana gasped in excitement.

"Does that mean I will have two birthdays?" Elizabeth lit up at the thought.

"Sprite, you will only have one birthday," Andrew informed her. He saw a pout forming and then added, "However, we will *always* celebrate the twentieth of June as the day that you joined our family." The pout disappeared before it could make its full appearance and was replaced by a bright smile.

"That is an excellent idea, Andrew," Uncle George agreed. "It will be such a hardship for my niece to have to suffer through more of the chocolate cake as we know she detests it!"

"Uncle George, it is Itch's job to tease me, not yours." Came the droll reply from his niece.

"Yes, that is my domain," Richard agreed with a grin.

"You know," Elizabeth again turned serious, "I feel like I was being selfish tonight."

"How so?" Aunt Anne asked.

"While worrying about how this will affect me, I forgot that Uncle Thomas and the rest of my birth family have been hurting since that insane woman had me removed from the nursery and ordered my murder," Elizabeth answered, feeling chagrined.

"You know that from now on they will be part of our family, do you not Lizzy?" Marie asked easily, as she had already started including them in her mind as such.
~~~~~~~

"If you heard your birth father's words, you will understand that he is doing what any parent would do, he is protecting you," Elaine stated. "Legally, as you are still a minor, he could demand your return to his home, but rather than do that, he considered the damage that would be done to you if you were ripped from the only family that you have ever known."

"Mother is absolutely correct," Andrew added gently. "If this had been months after you were taken, or even a year or two, there would have been no question, but now that you have been with us for almost fifteen years, it would do you far more harm than good to demand that you return to your birth family. I respect Uncle Thomas greatly as he put your best interests ahead of his own desires."

"Do not make the same mistake you made after Uncle Reggie was murdered, the same one your birth father was making tonight, when he attempted to take a burden on his shoulders that was not his to take," William told Elizabeth as he gave her a hug of support.

"You are a fine one to talk, Will," Richard smirked. "There is no one better than you at trying to take responsibility for that which is not yours!" Richard may have been ribbing his younger cousin, but all who knew William recognised that there was a lot of truth in the statement.

"Do not forget that after we all have had a night to absorb the miracle that happened here today, that we will be meeting at the Gardiners on the morrow to discuss the way forward," Aunt Anne offered.

"I am happy for you, Lizzy," Anne de Bourgh spoke for the first time in hours. "Even though your birth ... I truly do not want to say mother, as that demented woman does not deserve the title, so I will say birth woman. Even though her actions were despicable, you now have two families that love and care for you. In fact, you may be the luckiest woman in the realm rather than someone who was discarded."

"Will all of this not interfere with your coming out season, Anne?" Elizabeth asked her sister with concern.

"I do not believe so, especially if a certain gentleman is not obtuse," Anne replied coyly. "But that is a discussion for another time!" She exclaimed with finality as Elizabeth was about to ask more questions on the subject, and the collective inhales said others would too. She steadfastly ignored Aunt Anne, Marie, and Mother Elaine, as they were far more observant than the men who were now looking at her in surprise, concern, and confusion but for Andrew.

"You have to know that no one will push or pressure you, Lizzy. You may get to know your birth family at your own pace, and you will be the one to decide how much or how little of a role they will play in your life. We will support you no matter what you decide, even if you choose to go live with them in the future," Elaine told her daughter with all sincerity, although the thought of that eventuality hurt her heart. But just like her late husband had put their protection above his own, she would do the same for her daughter.

"You do not want me to go and live with the Bennets, do you, Mama?" Elizabeth asked, her look of hurt breaking her mother's heart anew.

"No, my darling daughter, you misunderstand; that is most certainly *not* my desire. All I am saying is that it is up to you and I will always love you, regardless of what you feel you must do. You are my daughter, and that will be so irrespective of where you reside." Elaine relaxed as she saw her daughter do so when she realised what her mother was actually saying, rather than what she thought she had heard.

"You will not be rid of me so easily, Mama," Elizabeth lightened the mood she had helped darken.

"Even were you to try to leave us, Georgie would just hunt you down and drag you back," William teased his cousin.

"And I would help her!" Richard added.

"It is time for the Darcys to go home, but if Georgie and Alex are sleeping upstairs, will you have someone escort them across the square in the morning?" Anne asked Marie.

"Of course, Aunt Anne," Marie waved off the question as they all knew the answer. "Or you can come back and break your fasts with us." After hugs from the Darcy men and a kiss from Aunt Anne, and a footman confirmed that the two younger Darcys were asleep, the three made the short walk across the square.

"What are the chances?" Anne asked as they walked toward home. "Not only the times that we know of that there has been contact or almost meetings, the Bingleys are Bennet tenants, and Lizzy has been playing chess with her father via the post for a long time now!"

"It is fate, Anne," George opined. "God works in mysterious ways."

"As long as my…eh hmm… our Lizzy does not get hurt," William added. He was glad that it was dark to cover his embarrassment at the slip, not catching the knowing look his parents shared.

~~~~~~~/~~~~~~~

Perry and Lady Rose arrived at Gardiner House before ten, after the note that they received requesting that they both attend the Bennets. After greetings, Jane explained why they had requested the meeting. "Papa has decided…" she started.

"With some prodding from his family," Bennet interjected.

"Well, perhaps a little suggestion was made, possibly," Jane allowed with raised eyebrows, "that it is time for the Bennets to purchase a townhouse…"

Lady Rose smiled and finished Jane's thought for her, "You would like to know if my townhouse on Grosvenor Square is truly for sale?"

"Yes, Lady Rose," Bennet responded, "Jane informed us that she believed you and Perry had discussed selling it."

"Jane was correct, and if you want it after you see it, it is yours," Lady Rose agreed.

"Thank you. Mayhap we will have time to view the house after we meet with our new family today," Bennet returned.

"With all the revelations yesterday, did you inform Mama that we have chosen a date for the wedding, Papa?" Jane asked.

"You did mention a date, did you not? I am sorry, Janey, with
~~~~~~~

everything that happened, my brain is a little addled so I forgot; what date have you and Perry chosen?" Bennet asked, somewhat embarrassed that he had allowed something that important to slip his mind.

"We chose Monday, the sixteenth day of January, Papa, as you stipulated that I must be eighteen before we marry. On that day, I will be older than eighteen," Jane challenged her father.

"I did say that, did I not? I have no objection to that date, do you, Tammy?" he asked his wife before giving final approval.

"No Thomas, I see no impediment to that date. Where do you want to marry from?" Tammy asked, knowing that with Perry's standing in society, he may want to marry from Town.

"Wherever my betrothed wants to marry will be perfect for me. So long as I am marrying Jane, I care not where," Perry gave his betrothed a look that reflected how besotted he was.

"I have always dreamt of marrying from Longbourn," Jane offered her preference.

"Then it is settled, we will marry from your home, my beloved fiancée," Perry said as he lifted her hands and kissed them. Just then the butler handed his master the morning papers.

Gardiner opened the paper and found the announcement of the engagement of the Duke of Bedford to Miss Jane Bennet of Longbourn. Lady Rose let a girl-like giggle escape. "My son does not let the grass grow under his feet, does he?" Bennet relayed how his soon to be son-in-law had the announcement ready in his pocket when he came to propose.

"Speaking of which, do you have time to discuss the settlement before the Fitzwilliams and Darcys arrive?" Perry asked, withdrawing a document from his pocket. "I would like Jane to be included if it is all the same to you, Bennet."

"Why am I not surprised that you arrived armed with a draft settlement? No, I have no objection to Jane being present. In fact, I was about to say that I would like my wife with me as well," Bennet responded and the four of them adjourned to Gardiner's study.

Before Perry could open the document, Bennet held up his

hand to gain the attention of the other three. "Tammy knows this, but Jane has a dowry that now stands at fifty thousand pounds thanks to my brother Gardiner, and she is also the owner of Netherfield Park."

"Papa, that is far too much! I thought my dowry was half that amount. You did not give me Lizzy's portion as well, did you? What about Netherfield for William or John?" Jane was concerned that she was getting too much, to the detriment of her siblings.

"Your concern is admirable, but all *three* of my daughters have a similar amount. They all started at the point you mentioned, but your uncle has done very well for us. As far as Netherfield goes, do not forget that your brothers are determined to forge their own paths. William will be ordained in a few short years and John would like to become a barrister. James has Longbourn and Tom Bennington Fields, so that only leaves Netherfield. As my oldest daughter, it is yours," Bennet laid out his reasoning, to which his wife had long agreed. "Both William and John have a legacy of twenty thousand pounds, well, that was what it was when I established it, though I am sure it too has grown, thanks to Edward."

Perry placed the document into Bennet's hands. As Bennet read, he let out a low whistle. "I knew you were wealthy, but I had no idea of the extent."

"It is not something we flaunt," Perry responded matter-of-factually. "With the two hundred and fifty thousand pounds I am settling on Jane, I have no need for her money or property. The final draft will state that whatever she brings to the marriage will remain under her sole control. There will be large portions settled on each daughter, and if we have more than one son, each will have an estate not part of the ducal entail and a large legacy as well."

"Papa, I want you to sell Netherfield," Jane was adamant. "I am sure that after so many years living as tenants, that the Bingleys would love to purchase it; I know they have been looking for an estate to purchase. I want none of the proceeds of the sale, whatever it is. I want it split between William, John, and Kitty." Jane had hardened in both tone and resolution, which told her parents that she was firm in her decision and would not be dissuaded.

"That is very generous of you, my daughter," Tammy was not surprised by Jane's generosity to her siblings but touched nonetheless.

"My dowry will be under my control, will it not?" Jane confirmed. Both Perry and her father nodded. "Then I want all the money from my dowry donated to Mama's charitable foundation."

"Jane, that is too much," Bennet started to say.

"No Papa, it is not!" Jane returned firmly. "Based on what I see here," she pointed to the draft settlement, "we are wealthy enough for many lifetimes, so I dare say that we will survive without my dowry and it will do so much good for those who have so little. I have five-thousand-per-annum pin money, for goodness' sake. Were I to get a new wardrobe every season in the most expensive of fabrics, I will never be able to spend that, never mind more!"

Bennet knew when it was time to withdraw from the field of battle. Perry noted the changes for his solicitor to amend the final draft and Bennet wrote a note to Oscar Bingley requesting that he attend him at the Gardiners' house that evening. He was about to send it when Gardiner told him that his wife suggested they invite the Bingleys for dinner that night, so Bennet wrote a new note.

~~~~~~~/~~~~~~~

At the same time, as members of the Ton were breaking their fasts, there was much wailing and gnashing of teeth as what they had all seen at Miss Bennet's coming-out ball but hoped what they were mistaken about was made official. The most eligible bachelor in the realm would not be theirs! Rumours abounded that, although the Bennets had eschewed Town, they had decent connections, but nothing exceptional. They were supposedly very wealthy, which had made the matchmaking
~~~~~~~

mamas nervous, so the only thing they had left to decry about the match was that she was a 'Miss' and was not titled. In the coming days, they were to find out that the Bennets' connections were far more than decent.

~~~~~~~~/~~~~~~~~

The courier had departed Gardiner House for Meryton with the dawn. The Phillipses were enjoying their morning meal when their housekeeper brought them an express and said that the Gardiner courier was waiting for a response. Hattie instructed that the courier be fed and relaxed in the kitchen until the master had written a response, then she and Franny looked at her husband expectantly.

"Hattie, you are not going to believe this," Frank stared at the missive with disbelief. He simply handed it to his wife, who let out a shriek of joy once she had read the most important part of the missive.

7 November 1796
Gardiner House
Portman Square, London

Brother and Sister,

I pray you are seated when you read this. We have been reunited with Lizzy!

This is not a joke; it is truly so! We suggest that you make haste and join us at Edward and Maddie's home.

Wait until you hear of all the coincidences.

Please DO NOT share this news with anyone else yet, other than the Hills, if you will; make a quick stop at Longbourn on your way.

Your brother,
Thomas

"Mrs Hester!" Hattie called at the top of her voice. "Please have our trunks packed, we depart for London as soon as may be. Sooner than may be if you can!" The housekeep bobbed a curtsey and left to instruct the maids. "Frank, I will write, telling them that we will arrive later *today*."

"I will pass it to the courier once you have finished, Hattie."
~~~~~~~~

Frank Phillips valued his life too well to even think about trying to gainsay his wife. Franny sat in stunned silence. She had heard about a cousin who had been stolen away, but never imagined that she would meet said cousin in her lifetime.

"Oh, I cannot forget to write a letter to Graham at Oxford," Hattie stated as she fluttered her handkerchief nervously on her way to the escritoire. The courier was on his way back to London but a half-hour later. The Phillipses were on the road within two hours with a quick stop at Longbourn, which produced tears of joy from the long-time housekeeper and, uncharacteristically, Mr Hill himself cried as he soothed his wife, the shadow of grief the elder Bennets and staff had suffered silently for so long finally gone.

~~~~~~~~/~~~~~~~~

The Bingleys were enjoying breaking their fast at their townhouse on Gracechurch street when a footman in Darcy livery delivered a note inviting them to dinner at Darcy House two days hence. The Hursts received an identical invitation around the same time, and both were accepted with pleasure.

As they were folding their napkins, the butler brought a second message from Gardiner House with an invitation for dinner that evening and it too was accepted. When Charles read the engagement announcement at breakfast, he found that he did not feel the regret he thought he would. He realised then that he had not truly been in love with Jane Bennet and wondered at her ability to understand him better than he had understood himself.
~~~~~~~~

CHAPTER 3

The Fitzwilliams and Darcys arrived at the Gardiner's house just after eleven. As everyone took seats in the large drawing room, there was an uncomfortable silence as no one wanted to be the first to speak. It was understandable that after a night to consider the occurrences of the prior day that there would be some reticence as no one from the newly extended families knew one another.

Perry and Lady Rose had left some minutes before as they felt that the families needed the time alone.

As she was the reason for the meeting, Elizabeth decided that she needed to break the ice. "Uncle Thomas and Aunt Tammy, what was I like before I was kidnapped from your home?" Elizabeth asked, assuming that it would be a subject that her birth father would be able to talk about easily.

"From the time you began to crawl, and you started early, it was like trying to catch the wind. You were a little whirlwind! Once you started walking, at about eight months of age, there was no stopping you. It was as if you went from crawling right to running, and once you started you did not stop," Bennet reminisced.

"My late Reggie and I, in fact, all of the family, called Lizzy our little whirlwind. I am happy to report that at Snowhaven, she was as she was when she lived with you," Elaine smiled the smile only parents can share when they love the same child.

"We all called her a whirlwind," Will contributed.

"Do not forget Sweetling and Sprite," Richard added with a grin.

"Lizzy was very intelligent; she started to talk early, although, as you found out, she had not mastered pronunciation yet," Bennet had a fond smile as he remembered his little Lizzy. "She loved me reading to her, and although she could not read, she always wanted to hold a book when I read to her, and one was never enough."

"One is definitely not enough even still today; do you have any idea what it is like trying to win an argument with one that remembers every word that she has read? She will take a position that she does not hold at times just to make the debate more interesting," William shared.

"I *am* here, you know!" Lizzy stated pertly.

"How could we forget, Sprite?" Richard drawled.

"Itch!" If her birth family was not there, she would have jumped up and chased her brother, but she decided to act ladylike, at least for a while longer.

"I believe there was talk of a chess match," George Darcy reminded the combatants.

"So, Darcy, you want to see me humbled by a young lady?" Bennet asked.

"Just as the rest of us have been when we tried to beat her!" came George's reply.

As if by mutual agreement, the two took up their positions at the board waiting for them in the corner of the drawing room. The rest of the family formed a semi-circle to watch the game, not just two years in the making, all knowing it was actually far more years than two. Andrew picked up both a black and white pawn, then mixed them behind his back and then offered Bennet the pick. He deferred the pick to Elizabeth, who chose white.

Someone had quipped about five minutes; but it did not even take that long. Bennet was amazed as he watched his second daughter wait for him to make his second move. From that point it seemed as if she had his number, knew what he would do before he did. He was fascinated as her eyes kept track of each piece on the board and how she would make her move the instant he removed his finger from his piece. In less than four minutes it was over.

"When we played by post, you did not have a board set up, did you?" he asked, but he was sure that he knew the answer before she gave it.

"No, Uncle Thomas, there was no board," she informed him almost apologetically.

"You remembered all in your head. Amazing!" Bennet had heard talk about her memory, but now he started to understand just how special Elizabeth was. "Have you read Romeo and Juliet?" he asked, and she nodded. "Act Four Scene One," he challenged.

Elizabeth gave him a look of 'that is too easy' and she started to recite:

Enter Friar Lawrence and Paris
Friar Lawrence
On Thursday, sir? The time is very short.
Paris
My Father Capulet will have it so,
And I am nothing slow to slack his haste.
Friar Lawrence
You say you do not know the Lady's mind.
Uneven is the course. I like it not.
Paris
Immoderately...

"Enough!" exclaimed Bennet, who took a moment to align his thoughts and turned to Will. "Yes, Will, I can see how trying to win a debate against my niece could be very frustrating."

"But well worth the challenge, Uncle Thomas," Andrew added.

The butler announced luncheon was served, and everyone walked into the dining parlour, sitting where ever they chose. Once they were served, Elizabeth turned to Jane. "Have you and my brother-in-law set a date for your wedding yet?" she enquired.

"We have, the day after I am eighteen, the sixteenth of January. We are marrying from our...I mean my home." Elizabeth did not comment on the slip. She saw that as Jane had been three at the time of her abduction, her older sister would have traumatic memories from that time that she at age one would not have had. "You will all come, will you not," Jane asked pleadingly.

"If we are invited, we will not miss it," Elizabeth stated.

"Not *if* Lizzy, *when*," Jane responded with finality. Elizabeth squeezed the hand of the woman who had once been the girl she had often seen in her dreams over the years.

An announcement and the wording thereof had been agreed upon between all of them earlier in the day and sent to the Times to appear on the morrow. The Bennets would no longer be unknown in Town after it was read by the Ton in the morning.

~~~~~~~~/~~~~~~~~

Mr and Mrs Phillips arrived just after the meal was over. Having seen the portrait of Bennet's mother many times, as soon as Hattie saw Elizabeth, she knew for certain who she was. Before introductions were completed, she marched up to Elizabeth, who was frozen in uncertainty, and enfolded the young woman in a hug while she cried tears of happiness. Aggie growled but stayed where she was, eyeing the person accosting her mistress. Luckily, Elizabeth had requested the footman looking after the huge dog outside, to bring her in to meet her new family. Lizzy patted the woman hugging her to show Aggie all was well. She nodded to the servant, and he led Aggie outside again, who assessed everyone in the room one more time before she followed.

"Your Aunt Hattie Phillips, my sister-in-law," Bennet said with a grin. "I think she is appreciative your beast did not have her as a snack."

"What a beauty!" Hattie exclaimed, as she took a step back from the young lady who had, but for the hand gesture to Aggie, stayed still. Thankfully, Hattie had not seen Aggie, or she would have had an attack of her infamous nerves.

When Elizabeth had recovered her equanimity after being soundly hugged by the kindly lady who she had never before met, her birth father made the official introductions. It was not long before Franny and Georgiana excused themselves to get to know one another better, as they were, but a few months apart in age. The story was told in abbreviated form for the Phillips;
~~~~~~~~

who then retired to their suite to rest from the trip.

'In the span of one day, I have gained three sets of uncles and aunts and a slew of cousins!' Elizabeth told herself. Yes, gaining a bigger family was definitely a huge positive, even if her newest aunt's manners were a touch on the vulgar side. Elizabeth felt that manners aside, she was a good person. They had just been invited to stay for dinner and the invitation had been happily accepted, so poor 'little' Aggie was sent home *sans* her mistress.

~~~~~~~/~~~~~~~

When the Bingleys arrived, they saw that the Fitzwilliams and Darcys were at Gardiner House, as were the Duke and Dowager Duchess of Bedford. Before they greeted anyone else, the Bingley parents offered profuse congratulations to the betrothed couple, then Charles Bingley stepped forward. Perry was prepared in case he said something to upset Jane as she had apprised him of Charles being an erstwhile suitor and his bitter words at her ball.

Most sincere wishes were offered and Charles apologised again to both, this time for his petulant words at the ball. Jane was pleased that she would not have to cut the acquaintance, and Perry too was pleased knowing that the man had behaved as a gentleman ought, thinking that the first minutes after a disappointment should earn anyone a little latitude. He would have been miserable had Jane rejected his addresses, so Perry had some insight most would not consider. Both the wishes and apology were accepted without reservation.

Martha heard Lady Elizabeth address Netherfield's landlord as 'Uncle Thomas.' "I did not realise that you are related to the Fitzwilliams," the confused matron stated.

"Neither did we until yesterday, Martha," Tammy told her as she took her arm.

"I do not understand." Martha was becoming more confused.

"We wanted to inform you of this when we invited you to dinner," Anne Darcy said, as she stood at Martha's other side.

"You know that we had a daughter stolen from us," Bennet reminded the Bingleys. All three nodded.
~~~~~~~

"You are aware that Lizzy was a foundling?" Elaine asked. Again, there were nods and then it hit all three Bingleys.

"Good Lord, Lady Elizabeth is the missing Bennet daughter!" Martha blurted out.

"After all these years, how, why, when?" Oscar asked, more than a little flummoxed.

"Many thanks to your son," Bennet grinned.

"What did I...oh, the chess games!" he realised.

"Yes, the chess games. We were to meet during the little season of the year that Papa was murdered. We chose to observe the mourning period at home, and so it was after a delay of almost two years we met yesterday," Elizabeth revealed.

"The portrait at Longbourn of Grandmother Bennet!" Charles exclaimed as he hit his head with his hand. "Some years ago, I told Louisa that it looked like Lady Elizabeth..."

"Elizabeth or Lizzy," the young lady interjected.

"Lizzy, but I never mentioned it to anyone else. I should have spoken up," he berated himself.

"There were many missed opportunities over the years, so please do not take yourself to task; you did nothing wrong!" Tammy laughed softly. "Otherwise, we all would have much more to blame as I myself asked Jane to not tell Thomas about the portrait, as I did not want to occasion him more pain." She had begged his forgiveness the night before and he had granted it, though made her promise that if they lost more children, she would tell him when she found portraits of their likeness in other people's houses.

"Is this why you asked us to visit today, Bennet?" Oscar Bingley asked. "Though either way we thank you for our inclusion of your familial happiness."

"No, Bingley, it is not just this, though thank you on behalf of the family on the Bennet side. Would you join Gardiner, Phillips, and me in my brother's study?" Bennet invited. At first Bingley was nervous but saw that Bennet was grinning, not the look of one who was about to deliver bad news, though it could be reminiscent of the news. He suddenly woke up to the fact that his landlord had said Phillips. He looked up and saw his friend walking toward him with Gardiner while Hattie was already bending his wife's ear. Bennet waited for him and they entered the study together.

Once the men were seated and Gardiner had poured them two fingers of his best French brandy, Bennet spoke first. "Have you found a suitable estate to purchase yet, Bingley?"

"We have seen a few, but none that had attracted our notice for a second look. If I am to uproot my wife and son, then it has to be something far better than Netherfield. I gave up asking you to sell to me some years ago," Bingley replied, as he took a healthy sip of the brown liquid.

"That was because I no longer owned Netherfield." Bennet grinned as he saw his friend's confusion. "I deeded it to Jane," he explained.

"So, Jane is our landlady now?" Bingley surmised.

"Technically yes, and without revealing personal information, my prospective son-in-law happens to be quite wealthy, so neither he nor Jane desire to keep Netherfield. In fact, my daughter has designated me her agent and directed me to sell the estate to a worthy buyer. Would you be interested..." Bennet was cut off.

"Yes, absolutely yes!" Bingley exclaimed, almost jumping out of his seat in his excitement at never having to quit Netherfield and to gain his impossible dream.

"And that is the main reason why we are included in this meeting of the minds," Gardiner indicated to himself and his brother, Phillips. "What is the market value, Phillips?"

"With the land that was annexed to Longbourn, it is worth a little more than eighty thousand pounds," Phillips replied.

Bingley was about to accept the price when Bennet lifted his hand. "Based on my instruction of how to disburse the proceeds, it is better for me if it were easily divisible by a factor of three, so what say you to five and seventy thousand pounds, old friend?" Bennet offered.

"Sold!" Bingley insisted. He could not wait to inform his wife, as it had been a long time that they had known that Netherfield Park was the only estate at which they would be truly happy. Phillips drew up an Intent to Purchase agreement with the final price. As soon as Bingley transferred the funds, Netherfield would be his. He was sorry that the Bank of England was already closed for the day, but he would present himself first thing in the morning and have the money deposited in the account Bennet had designated.

When the men returned to the drawing room just before dinner was announced, Bingley quietly approached Jane and thanked her sinserely for selling him her estate. She took much pleasure from the look of joy on Mr Bingley's face. She was also gratified that she had been able to increase William, John, and Kitty's portions.

Once they were seated, she leaned toward her betrothed, seated to her right, "It is done, Netherfield is sold."

"Did Mr Bingley purchase it, as you and your father suspected he would?" He asked, and Jane nodded her head in reply. There was no missing the joy on Mr Bingley's face, nor the fact that he was bursting to share the momentous news with his wife.

As she was enjoying the meal, Elizabeth thought back on how good it had felt when Jane hugged her the instant that she had been recognised as her long-lost sister. Each time they had greeted one another since that first lingering hug, either on arrival or departure, they hugged. It just felt right to Elizabeth, especially since she had recognised that Jane was the angel of her dreams over the years.

When Uncle Thomas had told of how he had felt something was wrong after the miscreant Wickham tried to murder her, she was amazed. However, when Jane told her of the dreams that she had, while at the same time Elizabeth was calling for her during her fever, Elizabeth had been shocked beyond belief. When she thought about it later, it explained why after so long of a separation, there seemed to be such a strong bond between her and Jane. For the while, she would be called cousin, but in Elizabeth's heart she felt the bonds of sisterhood as strongly as if she had been with Jane for the entirety of her life. To her great relief when she looked at her sister, Jane invariably turned and met her eyes and they shared smiles that proved they were both there together to their relief.

After dinner, separation of the sexes was eschewed, and the ladies were beseeched to provide music, and by design of the Darcy and Fitzwilliam families, Elizabeth was the final performer. Her newly reunited family all sat in awe and surprise as she played her first song, a Scottish ballad. Her final piece, an aria in Italian, was the one she truly enjoyed, and as her contralto voice swelled in song, there was absolute silence. After the song was completed, there was further silence for some seconds before the thunderous applause broke out. Even those who had heard her sing before had never heard her sing so well.

Bennet could hear that her Italian pronunciation and inflection was perfect. "Lizzy, do you speak Italian as well?" He asked.

"I do, Uncle Thomas, and a few others as well," she answered humbly.

"That is brown, Lizzy," Richard added. "A *few*! My sister has mastered most of the languages of which I am aware or have but heard of!"

"That may be because you have not heard of many languages, Richard," Will shot at his cousin.

"I would be careful if I were you, Will, unless you want to be pummelled again," Richard retorted in jest.

"Just how many languages are you fluent in, my dear?" Bennet asked, admiring the easy banter between the Fitzwilliams and Darcys.

"Nine," Elizabeth returned softly.

"Nine! Good Lord, what are they? I know of English and Italian so far." Bennet already knew that his second daughter was gifted, but as each additional layer as revealed to him, he was astounded all over again.

"French, German, Portuguese, Russian, Greek, Latin, and Hebrew," Elizabeth admitted.

"Why Hebrew?" Bennet enquired.

"I have some old copies of bibles in my library in that language and our Lizzy decided that she wanted to be able to study them so she learnt how to read it, then for good measure talk and read it," George Darcy offered.

"I hear that library of yours calling me," Bennet quipped. He turned back toward Elizabeth. "Are there any more hidden talents you have omitted to share, niece of mine?"

"Not that I can think of, Uncle Thomas," Elizabeth returned, still somewhat embarrassed at her accomplishments being a topic of discussion. "I suppose I am good at riding; I do love to ride Saturn and she is such a good horse."

"Again, Lizzy is downplaying her ability. She and that beast of a horse routinely outrun the rest of us, and there are a number of stallions in the group," Will proudly proclaimed.

"Why did you name her Saturn?" Bennet asked, astounded at another coincidence.

"Andrew started it," Elizabeth explained. "He named his stallion Orion because of the three stars on his forehead. I decided to use a celestial body as my big brother had, so when I saw the rings on her forelegs, I named her Saturn. Anne," she indicated her cousin with Perry and Jane, "chose the name Callisto for her mare." Then she added, "Gigi did not follow our lead, she named her mare Brown Beauty."

"It seems that it is another similarity between our families. My stallion is Jupiter; Jane's is Mars," seeing the questioning look Bennet clarified, "yes, Jane rides a stallion. My dear wife named her mare Neptune. Well, you get the idea. It may seem that my interests are restricted to chess and books; but I, in fact, have many interests—the study of celestial bodies being one."

Before they departed, Perry confirmed the Bennets would view the townhouse on the morrow at ten, as there had been no chance to do so during the day. It was not long after that everyone departed for their homes with plans made to meet on the morrow after the Bennets saw the townhouse.

~~~~~~~/~~~~~~~

As they crossed the threshold after arriving at their house,
~~~~~~~

Martha turned to her husband expectantly. "What is it that you are not telling us, Oscar? After the meeting in the study, you looked like the cat that got all of the cream, so I know it was not bad news."

"You are correct as ever, Martha, it was the *best* of news. Jane sold us Netherfield!" He informed his wife and son with glee just as they made it up the stairs, from the front door and into the drawing room.

"If that is a tease, then it a cruel one, Oscar. You know how much I love living at Netherfield!" she frowned.

He pulled out his copy of the signed-and-witnessed Intent to Purchase agreement to prove it was so; he was worried that his wife would suffer apoplexy, so great was her joy. She hugged her husband as the document slipped out of her hands and fell to the floor, where Charles retrieved it and read it.

"Wait, father, did you say that *Jane* sold it to us?" Charles asked.

"Yes son, Bennet gifted it to her. As her husband-to-be has more than enough wealth and properties, she chose to sell to help her brothers, who will not inherit one of the other estates and young Kitty," Oscar explained.

"The price is very good, father," Charles observed. "He could have asked up to one hundred thousand pounds!"

"You are correct, son; Bennet wanted a number that he could divide by three without too much trouble!" Charles suspected that they had received a 'friends-and-family discount' as ninety thousand was just as easy to divide by three.

As late as it was, the butler was still instructed to open a bottle of champagne, so that the Bingleys could toast their good fortune and their entry into the realm of landed gentlemen.

CHAPTER 4

Perry met the Bennets at ten in the morning. Before they ascended the stairs to the door, he pointed out Darcy House opposite and Matlock House, three doors down, on the same side of the square as they now stood. As they were about to enter, they spied Elizabeth returning from a walk in Hyde Park, being trailed by two enormous footmen, her companion, and with her huge dog Aggie trotting easily at her side.

Elizabeth, too, saw her brother-in-law and the Bennet family, so headed toward them. "Will he bite if we try to pet him," James asked nervously.

"No, Aggie is fully trained and *she* will do nothing until she detects someone trying to harm me, then she can be quite ferocious," Elizabeth explained to her cousin, well her brother but she was more comfortable thinking of the Bennet children as cousins, except for Jane.

"How old is she?" William asked as he joined James in rubbing behind one of Aggie's ears. Seeing his other brothers not being eaten by the pony-sized dog, John approached her and started to pet her around the tail which Aggie liked, so she turned and gave him a slobbering lick on his face. The rest of the party laughed as John pulled a face and tried to dry it off.

"She is a little past seven years old," Elizabeth answered once she had stopped laughing at her dog's antics.

"We are about to view Perry's townhouse to decide whether we should purchase it," Bennet informed his second daughter/niece. "You are most welcome to join us as we look over the house."

"I would like that," Elizabeth answered. She beckoned to her companion, a Mrs Annesley, and requested that she inform the family at Matlock House where she was. She asked John to take Aggie home, but Biggs remained with her, even knowing she was surrounded by family.

The housekeeper and butler were waiting for his Grace at the top of the stairs. Perry performed the introductions to the relatively new housekeeper and butler, Mrs Kerry O'Grady and Mr Jacob Franklin, who had been hired less than a year before when their predecessors retired. He explained that there were three maids and the same number of footmen as part of the skeleton staff maintained at the house.

As they were about to enter, Elizabeth pointed out Matlock and Darcy Houses. She was, of course, aware that the Bennets had been to her house the day of the revelation, but she was not sure that they knew how close they would be if they purchased the house.

"That is one of the reasons that this address is attractive, Lizzy," Bennet winked at her. "If we purchase it, then we will be able to keep an eye on you when we are all in town."

"More so I can keep an eye on you as you are less familiar with the ways of town, Uncle Thomas?" Elizabeth huffed, smiling when her Bennet family laughed.

Without seeing her, she sensed Jane next to her and turned to claim one of the warm hugs that Jane gave her. When they all followed Perry and the senior staff into the house, Jane and Elizabeth had their arms intertwined.

There was nothing not to like about the townhouse. From the outside, it looked like most of the others around the perimeter of the square, and Perry informed them that most of the houses on the square also had similar floor plans inside, except for one or two whose owners had made extensive changes. There were five floors, many family and guest chambers, an oversized ballroom, all the public rooms one would expect, a family and a guest sitting room, and three dining parlours; one for breakfast, an informal family parlour, and a large formal parlour. The ballroom and the three dining parlours could become one larger room to accommodate additional space for a ball.

After showing them where the master's and mistress's studies were, which had a connecting door, Perry had kept the best for last—the library. It was on the floor above the ballroom and was almost as big. At the instant that he saw all the tomes that had been undisturbed for far too long. Bennet made a decision; unless Tammy had objections, he would make an offer of purchase for the house. He asked Tammy to join him in the family sitting room close to the entrance to the library.

"Do you have any objections to us purchasing this town home, Tammy?" he asked as soon as he closed the door after he had kissed his wife soundly for the support, her smile proving she knew the house was important so he could be close to their new family.

"It was the library, was it not?" Tammy smiled. After thirteen wonderful years married to her husband, she knew him too well to doubt that was the case.

"Well, yes, I suppose that played a *small* part," Bennet teased his wife. "I like the house as a whole as it is close to our new family and but ten minutes by carriage to the Gardiners."

"No, Thomas, I have no objection whatsoever. On the purchase of this house, you and I are of one mind." Tammy kissed her husband to put an exclamation point on her statement.

"Well then, let us go tell our future son-in-law and see how his mother would like to proceed," Bennet said, kissing his wife again, the chaos of the last few days not tempering his need of reminding her she was paramount to his happiness.

"Perry, Tammy and I would like to purchase the house," Bennet announced as they joined the rest in the library. The three Bennet sons present expressed their approbation by laughter.

"Did I not say that once father saw the library, he would not leave this house without purchasing it," William smirked.

"None of us held a contrary view," John pointed out.

Jane and Lizzy used the occasion to hug, as they would be living close to one another while they were in town, well until Jane moved into Bedford House on Russell Square. The two were comforted by the fact that it was barely more than one mile from where they now stood. If that was too far, Perry owned a townhouse on St. James Square, which was even closer, not to mention the one on Portman Square that had been instrumental in their meeting.

"Before you meet with my mother and me, we require your word of honour on one point, Bennet," Perry stated cryptically.

"If you tell me what I will be binding my honour to, I will give you an answer," Bennet responded, trying to divine what Perry was driving at.

"The price that my mother will offer will be at or below market price. Her condition is that you accept the price with no argument," Perry revealed.

"Well, that is a promise I can make with ease. You have my word as a gentleman," Bennet responded. When the group descended to the entrance hall, Mrs Annesley was waiting for her charge. After she wished her family good luck for the upcoming meeting with the Dowager Duchess and her goodbye hug to Jane, Elizabeth and her escorts headed back to Matlock House.

~~~~~~~/~~~~~~~

That morning, the same members of the Ton who had placated their jealous feelings with the knowledge that Miss Jane Bennet had no remarkable connections, had to eat their words as they broke their fasts and read that day's copy of the Times. The recently unknown family had connections that anyone would envy. Not only that, but the royals had placed a congratulatory notice in the broadsheets, which was a clear signal to the Ton that the Rhys-Davies's royal cousins supported the match fully.

With both pieces of added information, there were none in the Ton who would commit social suicide by denigrating any of the Bennets, much less the Duke's betrothed. The family went from 'looked down upon' to one whom many wanted to ingratiate themselves to increase their own connections.

The kind of hypocrisy displayed by many in the Ton was the main reason Bennet had kept his family away from London society. Now, in the blink of an eye, hiding away in Hertfordshire had become an impossibility.
~~~~~~~

~~~~~~~~/~~~~~~~~

Bingley and his son walked into the main Bank of England branch as the doors were opened to the banking public. Oscar requested his personal banker, and within a minute or two he and his son were shown into the man's office. He handed the man Bennet's account information and then instructed him to transfer the required amount from his investment account into the one specified.

After verifying Bennets signature on the form, the banker filled out a transfer form, and after he had Mr Bingley's signature, he went to have the order executed. Not ten minutes later the man returned and handed Oscar the documents with the bank's official seal attesting the transfer had been made.

As they rode home Charles turned to his father, "Will not the outlay of seventy-five thousand pounds significantly hurt our income?" he asked.

"No son, it will not," Bingley saw his son's sceptical look. "Do you know how much Netherfield earns, Charles?" Bingley asked. His son shook his head. "It is just shy of four thousand per annum. So no, we will not suffer. In fact, it will be a few hundred pounds to our good."

"There will be those that call us 'new money' as we are new to the landed gentry," Charles pointed out.

"Let them say what they want, it will have no effect on us and those are not the type of people with whom we want to be acquainted!" Oscar reminded his son vehemently. They went directly to Gardiner House where they found Bennet was out with all of his family, save the twins. However, he had signed the deed in anticipation so once Phillips checked the transfer receipt and verified the account number, he had Bingley sign the deed as purchaser and he and Gardiner witnessed the document. The two Bingley men shook the brothers-in-law's hands vigorously, after which Oscar folded the deed carefully as if it was the most precious of gems.

From Gardiner House, Oscar went to his solicitor who made a copy of the deed for his client's record and locked the original in
~~~~~~~~

his safe until Mr Bingley returned home where he would place it in his own safe in his study.

When they arrived home, Louisa, Harold, and little Jane were present. There was much celebrating on Gracechurch Street that day!

~~~~~~~~/~~~~~~~

Bennet, Tammy, and Jane were shown into Bedford House on Russell Square. It looked to be at least twice the size of the townhouse that they had seen earlier in the day. The butler showed them into the mistress's study, which would be Jane's in a matter of months. Lady Rose was behind the nice-sized desk with Perry sitting on a settee off to the side. There were two chairs in front of the desk where Bennet and Tammy sat, while Jane joined her fiancé on the settee, sitting as close to him as propriety would allow.

"I understand from my son that my mother's house meets with your approval," Lady Rose smiled at her soon to be family.

"Indeed, Lady Rose, there was nought that we found fault with the home," Bennet informed her.

"Especially the library, Papa," Jane added importantly.

"It has only been a few days since we were reunited with Lizzy and here you are, displaying her reported impertinence. Where is the serene daughter I used to have?" Bennet teasingly asked his Jane.

"Perry did happen to mention how large your eyes became when they beheld the library, Mr Bennet. I am afraid that your hand was shown then." Lady Rose smiled.

"You do not know the half of it, Lady Rose," Tammy teased.

"Am I correct that you wish to purchase the old Winslow House and that you agreed to the terms that my son outlined to you when you made the decision," Lady Rose verified.

"On my honour, yes, I did," Bennet said. He was confused and then saw the lady with a wide smile on her face and froze, as it could not be but perfect, pleasure to gain such a smile from anyone.

"Please sign the deed, Mr Bennet," she indicated the pur-
~~~~~~~~

chaser's signature line.

Bennet's confusion grew. "But you have not mentioned price!" he exclaimed in exasperation.

"What has price to do with it?" Lady Rose challenged. "You agreed that you would not argue the price, did you not?"

"I did," Bennet admitted again, his suspicion that he had somehow been hoodwinked growing.

"Perry also guaranteed that the price would be at or *below* market, did he not?" she confirmed again.

"He did." Bennet knew that whatever the price, his honour was involved, so he would accept it and so signed in the indicated place. Lady Rose singed as the seller while Tammy, Jane, and Perry signed as witnesses.

"Perry, please deal with the money matters," Lady Rose instructed as she handed the deed over to the new owner.

"Do you have a Guinea on your person, Bennet?" Perry asked nonchalantly.

"I do...you are not selling me that property for one Guinea, are you?" a flabbergasted Bennet managed.

"No not selling, Bennet, *sold*!" Perry said with a big grin on his face.

"But..." Bennet started to object.

"You just confirmed that you would not argue the price, did you not?" Perry closed the coming argument.

"He did say at or *below* market, Thomas. You did not ask *how much* below," Tammy said with resignation, realising there was nothing to be done. They now owned a grand townhouse on Grosvenor Square for the price of one single Guinea!

"Please feel free to rename your house," Lady Rose suggested. "A Winslow has not resided there since before I was born, and besides it is yours now, so please name it what you will."

"Bennet House," Tammy suggested, and her husband nodded. "We will name it Bennet House."

"A fitting name," a smiling Lady Rose offered sweetly.

When Bennet looked at his daughter, he saw that there was no surprise on her countenance. "Jane Florence Bennet, did you know what your betrothed and his mother planned and you told us nothing!"

"Sorry Papa, I was sworn to secrecy, and as with yourself, my word is my bond," she replied without an ounce of repentance.

"This is how it begins, even before you are married, your allegiance is shifting," Bennet stated wistfully.

As if by magic, the Bedford House butler materialised from nowhere with five fully charged champagne flutes.

~~~~~~~/~~~~~~~

That evening when the families met at Matlock House, there was understandably much talk about the newly renamed Bennet House. There was understated excitement that the families would live so close, one to the other, when they were in Town.

It was not long before Marie, Elaine, Lady Rose, Maddie, and Anne Darcy volunteered their help if Tammy wanted anyone to go over the house with her, to make suggestions as needed, regarding redecorating. As the house had not been decorated since Lady Rose's grandmother's time, everything from cellars to attics would need attention. Tammy shared that once the decision to acquire the house had been made, she had authorised the housekeeper and butler to start interviewing servants.

After a lively family dinner, the men were in Andrew's study with cigars and drinks. Bennet pulled Perry to one side and simply asked: "Why?"

"After she gave up Netherfield to be sold to increase her sibling's portions, I knew that I wanted to gift her the townhouse and Mother agreed wholeheartedly. When I discussed it with her, she refused, and that is when I considered the neighbourhood and had the idea to offer it to your family. Mother seconded the idea and only then did I tell Jane, as I did not want her to think that I was going behind her back. She too added her approval to the scheme," Perry related.

Noting that the young duke had not mentioned the plan to ensure he agreed not to fight the price, Bennet made an educated guess. "It was Jane, was it not?"

"What was Jane, Bennet?" Perry chuckled.
~~~~~~~

"Do not be so obtuse with me, Perry, you know what I mean. Jane suggested the ruse so that I would not object, as she knew that I would never accept such a gift without having no option," Bennet surmised, fairly certain he was accurate in his assessment.

"Please do not censure her for it." Perry did not think that Bennet would, but he wanted to be sure. "Even though it was her suggestion, it was I who executed the plan."

"Make yourself easy, Perry. I know how generous my daughter's heart is. Unless, of course, you ever make the mistake of running afoul of her. It is then one discovers that she can be quite strident when pushed to it. Jane would take the gown off her back and give it to someone whose gown was soiled if she could find a way to do it and still maintain propriety. That is why I guessed that it was her suggestion." Perry relaxed as Bennet assured him Jane would not know that her father was aware it was her idea to make sure he could not refuse.

When the men returned to the drawing room, they arrived at the tail end of the ladies making plans to visit the modiste. "Thank you, Mama," Georgiana said as she kissed her mother on the cheek. "This is the first time that I will go to the modiste," she effused.

"Do not forget, Georgie, that it will only be two dresses, a day dress and gown for Perry and Jane's wedding. In a year or two, you will have more dresses made by Madam Chambourg," Anne told her daughter.

"Andrew, while you were out, we were talking. What think you of the De Melvilles and Ashbys being informed as to the true nature of the Bennet's relationship to us? We do expect Ian Ashby to be calling after he returns from Surry. I do hope the problem that called him to his estate was not serious," Elaine hoped.

"I have no objection as long as Uncle Thomas has none," Andrew replied. The relationship to both families was explained to Bennet.

"There is no objection from either of us," Bennet responded

after a quick glance with his Tammy. The benefits of such an intuitive wife were innumerable.

~~~~~~~/~~~~~~~

It was a few days later when George Wickham found out why his employer had thrown the London papers down in disgust and stormed off to her chambers. As if they did not have enough connections already, now some long-lost relations of the Fitzwilliam and Darcys had been discovered; of course, they were wealthy too, and their daughter was marrying the Duke of Bedford! Life was just not fair!

He had hoped that at least Hodges would do some good and make both families suffer after the Earl's murder, but it seemed that they were living well again while he was stuck in this nowhere town under the thumb of Mrs Fitzpatrick. They just kept on getting more while he had nothing; less than nothing.

He had thought that the old lady would have an apoplexy when the news about the triumphant coming out of Miss Anne de Bourgh as the ward of the Earl of Matlock had been reported. What made George Wickham want to throw caution to the wind and ride to London to dispatch his half-sister, was when he read that it looked like she was being courted by an 'IA'. He did not know or care who that was, but he did know enough that if she married, any chance he had of claiming Rosings would be dead.

There was but one thing that held him back, how would he be able to prove that he was the son of Sir Louis de Bourgh? He acknowledged that without that information he would have no claim whether his half-sister lived or died. He even considered snatching her and whisking her off to Gretna Green, then making her disappear as soon as Rosings Park was his, but he quickly eliminated that as a viable plan. If he showed his face, married or not, he would end up at the end of a hangman's noose.

He did not know how he would achieve his aims of gaining Rosings or dispatching the mongrel, but he would keep trying to determine a way to achieve all his goals while ruining all of their plans.

~~~~~~~/~~~~~~~

Martha Bingley had to pinch herself from time to time to remind herself that she was not dreaming. They were landowners. It hit her while she was savouring the thought that she had achieved all the things that she used to aspire to and pretend that she had, all without having to climb over anyone to get there.

Her darling granddaughter had just turned two and was the apple of her grandmother's eye. Louisa was increasing again, the Hursts hoping for a son to continue the line and inherit Winsdale after her son-in-law, hopefully, many years from now.

Martha had written to Sarah Lucas, Cheryl Long, and Jenny Goulding to inform them that they would never be leaving the neighbourhood as they were now the owners of Netherfield. Tammy Bennet, Hattie Phillips, and Maddie Gardiner had accepted invitations to tea for that morning, and Martha was looking forward to seeing her friends.

Once Charles had admitted to himself that he was not really in love with Jane Bennet, it helped him to become far more introspective. He finally realised that he had been in love with her beauty, not the person Jane had grown into. He promised himself that he would start looking at character and compatibility first, and then after he would consider the looks of the young lady. He needed to be sure when she looked at him, she saw him as the man that he would be with her at his side. He was nothing compared to Darcy or Perry in looks, but the woman who looked at him to fill her dreams was the one he would be able to make happy without regret.

Oscar Bingley was sitting in his study going over the numbers for the three Bingley Carriage works, for they had added the third some two years previously in Liverpool. He suddenly felt a sharp pain in his left arm and tried to ignore it, then it hit him a second time and this time it was in his chest too. He felt like his heart was about to explode and then Oscar Bigley's world went black and he slumped forward onto his desk.

CHAPTER 5

Martha could not understand what was keeping her husband. By the hour of ten, at the latest, he was in bed with her every night since the day they were married. He had asked not to be disturbed in his study that evening, but now Martha was concerned. She rang for her maid, asking her to send her husband's man to the study to make sure that the master was well.

Fifteen minutes later, her maid returned and Martha knew that something was very wrong by her maid's pallor. Before the maid could speak, her son burst through the door, tears rolling down his cheek. "F-father has passed," he managed, as he went to comfort his anguished mother, who had started to wail. "I have sent for the doctor, Mama. Should I send a note to Louisa and Harold?" he asked gently.

"No, Charles," his mother managed through her crying. "Louisa needs to sleep in her condition, and it will accomplish nothing tonight," she blew her nose and wiped her eyes, then thought of her pregnant daughter, and realised that she had to be strong at this moment to honour her husband the way he deserved; later there would be time for grieving. "We will notify them and our friends on the morrow. You are the head of the family now, Charles. I know that you are not yet three and twenty, but there is no choice and you know I will guide you as I have been part of your father's considerations in these last years."

"I know, Mama, but I cannot think about that now. He is still warm in his study," Charles lamented.

"He was the love of my life, my son. After I changed my course those years ago, we became as close, if not closer, than we were when we married. I will mourn your father for the rest of my days, but I do know that he would want us to carry on and not stop living. Yes, once these initial things are done, you are right, there is time to grieve. Let me dress and I will meet you in the drawing room." Martha gave her son a kiss on his cheek and asked him to send her maid back in, as she had left the room when Master Charles had entered it.

Charles was sitting with his head between his knees when his mother entered the drawing room some twenty minutes later. The physician arrived and was taken to examine the body. About ten minutes later, Mr Morrison entered the drawing room. "My condolences to both of you," he said with a bow. "There was nothing that could be done for Mr Bingley by either myself or you."

"Do you have a guess as to what took my husband as he was not yet fifty?" Martha asked in as steady a voice as she could manage.

"Based on what I saw, and the fact that his hand was clutching his chest as he passed, I believe that Mr Bingley suffered a heart attack," the doctor surmised. "As it is cold, I had the servants carry the body to lie in the sickroom near the study. What are your plans for burial?" he asked.

"We have not yet made any plans," Charles spoke up, straightening his spine as he met the eyes of the doctor. "We live in Hertfordshire; we will take my father home on the morrow or the next day, and he will be laid to rest in Meryton."

"I am sorry that there was not more I could do. I left the certificate of death on the desk, after the body was removed from the study," Mr Morrison informed them.

After he repeated his condolences to the widow and her son, Charles walked the doctor to the front door. When he returned, his mother stood. "I am going to sit with my husband." She stated, and with that, she took determined steps toward the sickroom where his body lay.

~~~~~~~~/~~~~~~~

After a scant few hours, Charles woke from a fitful sleep. He hurried his man through his morning ablutions and went to the
~~~~~~~~

sick-room without stopping for his morning cup of coffee. There he found his mother sitting in the cold room holding her husband's cold hand. "Mother, you will not be able to help anyone if you make yourself sick from lack of rest," Charles was gentle as he helped his mother to rise, requesting a footman summon his mother's lady's maid. When she arrived and curtsied to the new master and her mistress, Charles asked her to assist his mother upstairs to wash and rest. He was firm that she needed to rest for at least four hours and that she would have something to eat when she woke.

Charles Bingley had just truly assumed his role as head of the Bingley Family. There was a hole in heart his father had filled, but his mother's words had guided him as now was truly not the time to indulge his sorrow. There was much to do. "I will miss you every day, Papa," he told his father's body as he sat with it for a minute. "And as much as I want to stay here with you, there is much I need to achieve this morning." He stood, leaned over and kissed his father's cold forehead, then instructed the footman to stand watch at the door.

He went to the study and started to write a note to Louisa, then stopped himself and tore it up. He could not deliver this devastating news by missive. After he took care of the missives he did need to write for both business and extended family, he would ride to their house on Grover Street to see Louisa and Harold.

He knew that these notes had to be legible and without blots. Truth was, when he desired, he could write as clearly as the next man, but he normally rushed and let his thoughts fly hither and yon, producing the ever-famous messes that were nigh on unreadable. His first note was an express to the Nichols to open Netherfield and place the signs of mourning. The next was to Mr Pierce, who in addition to the Longbourn living held the one at the church in Meryton so that he was aware that his services would be needed for the funeral service and interment.

Charles had considered taking his father back to Scarborough to rest with his family there but quickly rejected that in favour of Meryton. He knew how proud and happy his father had been at finally becoming a landed gentleman, and the friends they had made were now closer to them than most family, so Charles determined that Oscar Bingley would arrive at the estate that he now owned, before being laid to rest for his eternal slumber.

Next, he wrote to Uncle Paul and the family in Yorkshire, also to be sent by express. He told his uncle that the funeral would be in ten days so that they would have time to make the journey to pay their last respects to the oldest Bingley. Last, he sent black-edged notes to the Darcys, Bennets, Gardiners, Phillips, and Fitzwilliams. Once he was finished, he knew that he could no longer defer the inevitable, breaking the news to his older sister…as the sun now told him it was morning.

When he was shown into the breakfast parlour, Louisa was happy to see him until she noticed the black armband. "Charles, who?" she asked as her husband stood to support his wife.

"Papa," Charles replied simply.

"When?" Louisa asked, as she sunk into her chair, tears flowing down her face in the initial stages of shock.

"Last night. Mama did not know why he had not come to bed, so she sent his man to the study to check on him and he found our father," Charles shared sadly.

"Why am I only being told now?" Louisa asked angrily.

"Mother said, and I agreed with her, that there was no reason to wake you and disturb your rest," Charles explained to placate his sister.

"I think that was a wise decision, Lulu," Hurst opined as he hugged his wife to himself.

"Come, Harold, let us get ready to go to Gracechurch street. I want to see my Papa," Louisa was determined.

"I rode here on my horse, so I will see you back at the house. Father will be moved to Netherfield tomorrow; and I have already sent out the notices. If you feel that Harold's parents should be notified, I will leave that to you as I did not send them a notification," Charles informed his sister then took his leave for the solitary ride back to the house in which he would never hear his father's voice again.

~~~~~~~/~~~~~~~

Andrew had just approved Ian Ashby's application to court his sister Anne de Bourgh. Ashby had a small estate, Sherwood Park, not far from Rosings over the Kent-Surrey border. He also had a healthy legacy that was bequeathed to him by his maternal grandmother along with the estate. Andrew had no concerns that his friend was a fortune hunter. He had just summoned Anne to congratulate her when the butler offered the salver to master. Andrew paused; his stomach sank as soon as he saw the black edging.

"If they do not already know, I give you leave to inform mother, Marie, and Lizzy. I see I have some business I cannot delay, but I will join you soon," he said to Anne as he stood and gave her a hug. "Always treat my sister like the beloved gift that she is, Ashby," Andrew warned.

"If Anne agrees to marry me in the future, you have my solemn oath that she will never be treated as anything less than she deserves to be," Ashby intoned seriously as he followed Anne out of the study.

Andrew lifted the missive and held it carefully, as if he thought it would bite him. He did not recognise the script, so he breathed a breath of relief. He was relatively sure that it was not a family member, but then he realised that he was not familiar with any of his new family's handwriting. He finally opened it, as all of the guessing in the world would not reveal the contents to him.

He read in surprise that Mr Oscar Bingley had passed away the night before and would be buried in Meryton, Hertfordshire at the Church of St. Alfred on Thursday, the first day in December. His sympathies went out to the Bingleys, but at the same time he felt relief it was not a member of his extended family. Now intimately familiar with the after-effects of losing a father, he quickly sent Bingley a note to call upon him for any reason and went to tell his family. When Andrew entered the family sitting room, Marie saw the black edged missive in his hand.
~~~~~~~

"Who?" she simply asked.

"Mr Bingley passed away last night," he announced, "he will be laid to rest in ten days at his home."

"The Bingleys are neighbours to my birth family, are they not?" Elizabeth asked.

"Yes, Sprite, you are correct. In fact, until a few days ago Uncle Thomas was his landlord. Mr Bingley just purchased the estate," Andrew replied. Without saying it, they all knew that Lizzy would be returning to the area from where she was kidnapped earlier than any of them had expected, but she would not be alone. All of her family would be there with her.

"Where will we stay?" asked Marie. "Or will we just go the day of the funeral?"

"I will walk across to Darcy House and ask Uncle George if he would like to join me in riding to Gardiner House to consult with our new family," Andrew decided.

Just like the announcement of Perry's and Jane's betrothal had been overshadowed, so was for the news of Anne's courtship. But like Jane before her, she begrudged no one, as most certainly the other news of the day took precedence.

Andrew was ushered into his uncle's study where in addition to his uncle, he found his aunt and cousin Will already present. All three looking as grim as he felt. He saw the opened black edges note on his uncle's desk. "It is a very sad day for the Bingleys. I assume, like us, that you will be attending the funeral and spending time with the family, especially as Will and Bingley are so close." Andrew waited for his answer.

"Yes, we will, but we do not know if there is a decent inn in the town? We will not impose on the Bingleys at a time like this," George stated firmly.

"You have my full agreement in that, Uncle George, but did you forget that we have a new family who lives in the area? I was going to ride over to talk to Uncle Thomas, get from him a list of options for Meryton. Would you like to join me?" Andrew suggested.

"I will. What about you, Anne, Will?" George looked to his

wife.

"My place is with my friend to support her. I will change into a more sombre dress and then order the carriage for Gracechurch Street," Anne stated resolutely.

"I will join Mother," Will said. "Bingley will need someone to be there for him."

With the decisions made, George Darcy called for his horse and the two men rode the short distance to Portman Square. As they arrived, they saw a carriage in front of the house, and shortly after Maddie Gardiner, Tammy and Jane Bennet, and Hattie Phillips descended the stairs, all dressed in sombre attire. They greeted the two arriving men, and as soon as the door was closed the carriage rocked into motion, conveying the ladies to the Bingley residence in support of their friends.

They were shown into Gardiner's study where the three brothers-in-law were in discussion. "We met your wives on their way to the Bingleys as we arrived," Andrew stated, "Aunt Anne and Will were departing for Gracechurch Street just after Uncle George and I rode here," Andrew explained.

"We did not want to impose on the Bingleys and seek to be hosted at Netherfield; is there a good inn in Meryton?" George asked.

"Stuff and nonsense," Bennet huffed. "We are family, and not only do we have many chambers at Longbourn, but Bennington Fields's manor house is available and is larger than the house at Netherfield. No, you will not be staying at the Royal Crown, you will be welcome with us for as long as you wish to stay," Bennet informed them all in a tone that brooked no opposition.

"That being the case, on behalf of Anne, my children, and myself, you have my thanks Bennet," George inclined his head.

"The same for the Fitzwilliams," Andrew added.

"It is not completely altruistic," Bennet quipped. "Now you will have no option but to invite me to Pemberley to see your fabled library, Darcy." Even though it was a day to be sad, the men grinned. "We three are about to join the ladies at the Bingley's town home, will you join us?"

It was decided that George would ride with Bennet and his brothers, and that Andrew would lead his uncle's horse home to collect Marie and his mother, and join the rest to comfort the family. As they prepared to leave, Bennet could not but think about the fact that Lizzy would be back at Longbourn for the first time in close to fifteen years. While the catalyst was the worst of the reasons, he could not repine at the thought of her joining them at her home, which Longbourn always was and would always be.

When Andrew, Marie, Richard, and Elaine arrived at the Bingleys, the ladies were in the large drawing room comforting Martha and Louisa. Marie and Elaine joined them after expressing their condolences to the two ladies in mourning garb. Andrew and Richard, who had asked for the rest of the day off from his general when the messenger from Matlock House brought him the news, joined the men in the smaller parlour.

After the brothers expressed their sympathies to Bingley, Richard gave his friend a brief hug. "I was just telling the rest of the gentlemen that we will depart at first light on the morrow to take my father home to Netherfield," Charles informed the Fitzwilliams.

"We, too, will depart tomorrow," Bennet stated, speaking for him and his two brothers.

"I thought, Andrew," George claimed Andrew's attention, "that we should wait two days to give our hosts time to prepare to be invaded by Darcys and Fitzwilliams."

"There is no need to delay unless you need to," Bennet interjected before Andrew could respond. "I sent expresses to the housekeepers at both estates before we departed Gardiner House, so all will be prepared before we arrive home on the morrow."

"If you are sure, Uncle Thomas," Andrew verified.

"Completely." Bennet showed the same firmness he had taken on when he insisted that he host his new family, so there was no further argument.

"In that case, what say you, Uncle George? We will depart tomorrow after we break our fasts?" Andrew asked, and his uncle nodded in approval.

"I apologise, Bingley," Richard frowned as he looked at his long-time friend. "I will not have leave until two days prior to the funeral, so I will be there after the rest of my family."

"Please do not make yourself uneasy, Richard," Charles waved that aside, "I understand completely as your time is not your own. I am rather grateful that you were even able to come today."

Bennet watched Charles Bingley with a keen eye; and he liked the changes that he marked. The irresolute and somewhat immature boy was gone, and in his place was a man; a man who had been forged in the fire of his grief, one who knew his own mind and would not defer to others. He had asked for advice, but he owned his decisions. Bennet saw some irony in the change in his neighbour. If he had been this version of himself prior to Jane meeting Perry…who knew what would have been for he would have approved of this man for his Jane; the boy he had been was gone.

"Andrew, would you come see me this evening? I need to discuss something with you," Bennet asked quietly so as not to arouse everyone else's attention once he remembered that he needed to talk to Andrew and did not want to defer the conversation any longer.

Jane was sitting in the drawing room with her friend, comforting her as best she could while Tammy sat on one side of Martha and Hattie the other. Martha was gratified that so many of her friends had come to give her their full support. As sad as she was, she knew that she would not be going through this horrid time on her own with just her immediate family. Charles had confirmed that he had sent notices to her widowed mother and siblings, and she was confident that they would join the Bingleys who were travelling from Scarborough. On hearing this Tammy quietly offered to host any of their family at their two estates if they did not have space at Netherfield.

~~~~~~~/~~~~~~~

Other than Tammy and Hattie, the rest of the friends re-
~~~~~~~

turned to their homes that evening. Those two would not leave their friend alone to sit vigil on her own during the long night that was to come.

Andrew was shown into the study at Gardiner house where Bennet, Gardiner, and Phillips were waiting for him, and sat in the available chair. "Before I get to the subject that I wanted to talk to you about, I need to ask; how is Elizabeth feeling about the prospect of being at Longbourn again, or would you be more comfortable at Bennington Fields?" Bennet asked. "I will tell you now, we have informed our closest friends, and our housekeeper, and butler, so they do not think that Lizzy is the spectre of my late mother come to haunt them."

Andrew was actually relieved that the friends had been informed. The last thing Lizzy needed was a bunch of strangers staring at her.

"The subject was canvassed with her, and she has no objection to us being hosted at Longbourn as she has no bad memories associated with the house. The people who caused the trauma of rending her from you are no longer alive, and so the evil is buried in the past," Andrew responded.

"I told you that it would not be an issue, Bennet," Phillips said smugly.

"It did not mean that I did not have to ask the question," Bennet shot back.

"Gentlemen, could we return to the matter at hand?" Gardiner rebuked his brothers.

"Yes, I want to transfer Lizzy's dowry for you to add to hers, if you're willing," Bennet informed Andrew bluntly.

"She already has a dowry of fifty thousand," Andrew said.

"That is from your family, this will be from her birth family. When she was a babe, I established a dowry of five and twenty thousand pounds for Lizzy to match Jane's. Thanks to Edward here," he indicated over his shoulder to where Gardiner stood, "it has more than doubled and stands at just under five and fifty thousand pounds," Bennet stated. Andrew almost smiled when he saw the determined look he had seen before, now in no doubt of where Lizzy got her stubbornness.

"Then on behalf of Lizzy, I thank you, Uncle Thomas," Andrew said graciously.

Phillips presented papers for Andrew to sign, then presented Andrew with a draft for the full amount. Andrew promised he would deposit the funds in the morning prior to their departure for Meryton.

~~~~~~~~/~~~~~~~~

Just after sunup, the sombre convoy departed Gracechurch Street. The undertaker's coach led the two Bingley family carriages, which were followed by the Bennet, Gardiner, and Phillips' conveyances. Three hours later, after a stop at the Bank of England to deposit the funds into Lizzy's dowry account, the Fitzwilliams and Darcys too headed toward Hertfordshire.
~~~~~~~~

CHAPTER 6

Elizabeth felt her excitement growing as the carriage traversed the town of Meryton. She recognised nothing, but each turn of the carriage's wheel brought her closer to the place where she had been born. Uncle Thomas had explained that the house was nothing like when she had lived there; it had been rebuilt and enlarged a few times over what it had been then, but it was still the place where she entered the world, and she could not wait to see it.

Georgiana and Anne were seated on either side of her, Andrew and Marie opposite. Her mother was riding with the Darcys on the last leg of the short trip from town. Marie was knitting and Andrew looked like he was sleeping. True his eyes were closed, but he was very much awake.

He was missing his late father, especially today of all days as he would have loved to have seen where his beloved daughter had begun her life. He thought back to the afternoon before they were informed of Mr Bingley's death when he and Marie, along with Perry and Lady Rose, had met with the De Mellviles and Ashbys. Once he had disclosed the true relationship to the Bennets, no one had been overly surprised. When they read the notice, both had suspected that there was more to it than the 'long-lost relatives' mentioned in the announcement.

Lady Rose suggested that she be authorised to disclose the truth of the connections to her cousins. After discussing the pros and cons, Andrew and Marie had given their permission, agreeing that the Queen would be unhappy to hear this news from the papers or a third-party source.

The decision had proved to be the correct one. The following day while everyone was condoling with the Bingleys, Lady Rose had met with her cousin at Buckingham House. The Queen had expressed her full-throated support if and when needed, and had been most appreciative that she had been informed before it became general knowledge. The Queen had also sent a note to the Bennets congratulating them on the betrothal of their one daughter to her cousin Perry and for being reunited with their daughter, Lady Elizabeth.

Lady Rose had reported that the Queen had been most impressed with the way that Mr Bennet had approached the situation, particularly his unwillingness to uproot his daughter's life a second time. Andrew's reverie was broken as the vehicle came to halt under the portico of a large and new looking manor house. From the servant's carriage came a series of indignant 'woofs' from Aggie who thought she should be included in everything that her mistress did. Thankfully, the Bennets had no problem with Aggie accompanying the family into Longbourn and had given permission for her to sleep in her normal place, on the mat next to Elizabeth's bed. James and Tom were vastly pleased that Aggie was at Longbourn as they had already fallen in love with their cousin's enormous hound.

Elizabeth felt her heart quicken as the Bennets all stood to welcome her to her birth home. The coach with her mother and the remaining four Darcys was right behind them, so by the time Andrew handed her out, they had all alighted from their conveyance.

"Welcome to Longbourn siste…er…I mean Cousin Lizzy," Kitty welcomed her, first though stumbling over the relationship.

"Thank you, Kitty," Elizabeth took her hands, "I know this is all very confusing, but the salient point is that we *are* family."

"Hear hear," Bennet seconded his second daughter's sentiment. "I welcome all of you to our home. Let us go inside, I am sure everyone would like to refresh themselves after travelling." There was a chorus of agreement and Tammy led the guests into the house while one of the footmen took Aggie for a walk to stretch her legs. As they gained the entrance hall, there was a gasp off to the side.

"Oh, she is so beautiful. She is the very image of your mother, Master," blurted out a tearful Mrs Hill, and her husband stood next to her, his eyes suspiciously moist.

"Everyone, this is Mrs Hill our housekeeper who has been at her post since before Jane was born," Tammy made the introduction. "Next to her is Mr Hill, our butler."

"Please pardon me, Lady Elizabeth," Mrs Hill's embarrassment at her outburst was obvious. Before she could complete what she wanted to say, the beauty who looked as if she had jumped out of the portrait in the gallery, ruby-encrusted cross and all, approached the housekeeper and took her hands.

"Nothing to pardon, Mrs Hill. I am just as excited to see Longbourn and everyone here, likely even more so. It is very good to meet someone else who knew me as a babe." Elizabeth put the nervous woman at ease.

"Master, Miss Browning requested that she be allowed to meet Lady Elizabeth, if possible," Mrs Hill requested. At Elizabeth's questioning look, her birth father explained.

"Loretta Browning was the other nursemaid who was looking after you alongside Tammy when that..., eh hm, she too was drugged the night you were taken. She now works for our parson Mr Pierce and his wife Miss Charlotte Lucas as was. They have a daughter Emma, born in May of this year. As we have no more little ones, when Charlotte was looking for a nursemaid, we suggested Miss Browning," Bennet explained.

"I will be happy to meet her," Elizabeth informed the housekeeper who smiled in pleasure at the confirmation.

Tammy showed her guests to their chambers rather than giving that task to Mrs Hill. There had been a debate whether to place the guests in the family wing or the guest wing. In the end, Tammy and her husband had decided on the guest wing as they did not want to push too hard. It was important that the pace Lizzy determined would be the pace they would follow.

Soon after everyone had been shown to their rooms everyone met in the largest drawing room. On the way down Elizabeth had stopped in the gallery with her family and they had all marvelled at how much she resembled her Grandma Elizabeth, who was called Beth, Bennet. Her Uncle Thomas had previously explained that he had named her after his late mother. At the time, he had gone into depth about *that* women's mania and how she had wanted Lizzy placed with a tenant family, but thankfully her presence had long been excised from Longbourn. During that discussion, she had learned that even her new Uncle Edward and Aunt Hattie spoke as if they were the only Gardiner children.

Once everyone was comfortable, Tammy rang for tea which was accompanied by freshly baked pastries and slices of chocolate cake. Bennet did not miss how Lizzy was eyeing the chocolate cake and chuckled as he nodded at the marvel of how some things never change. "It was your favourite, you almost made yourself sick demanding a second slice on your first birthday," he remembered fondly.

"That never changed," Elaine recounted. "Every birthday cake since she came to us had to be chocolate, the bigger the better, and she has had two slices each and every year!"

"And never got sick," Andrew added with a grin.

"It was not only birthdays, for any family celebration at Matlock House or Snowhaven, the bakers knew that no matter what else was ordered that there would have to be a chocolate cake," Elaine smiled widely.

"Mama! You are making it sound like I indulge in gluttony!" a scandalised Elizabeth responded.

"Kitty and I must take after you, Lizzy," Tom grinned, "we both love chocolate cake and would have it for every meal if Mama would allow it, but," he affected a fake pout, "she will not."

"We all like chocolate cake," William spoke up, "just not as much as Tom and Kitty!" Kitty stuck out her tongue at her oldest brother.

"Nothing remains from the house that I was born in, is that correct, Uncle Thomas?" Elizabeth asked.

"That is a fact," Bennet agreed. "It was not just the bad memories; over the years my ancestors had added to the house in a hodgepodge manner. Rather than perpetuate the same mistake I had the house torn down and rebuilt from scratch. Tammy will tell you that I considered a renovation, but we saw the folly of it and chose the harder route which was really no hardship as we had another residence nearby."

"We do have your bed, and the clothing which was left after you were stolen from us," Tammy informed Elizabeth. "Would you like to see them?" Elizabeth nodded, blinking rapidly to either allow the tears in her eyes to fall or fade. Tammy led Elizabeth and the Fitzwilliam and Darcy women up to the nursery. It was large with a number of doors that led to nice sized chambers for the servants that worked with the children, and there was one door that was kept closed until today.

Tammy opened it to reveal a small bed, that of a toddler's, a blanket folded neatly at the foot of the bed, and two shelves with tiny outfits on it. Elizabeth slowly walked to the little bed and sat on it, caressing the blanket that laid protective over it. She lifted each little outfit and admired her clothing from so many years ago and there was not a dry eye among the women watching her.

Even with her memory, she could not summon any which included the items in the room. She folded each item neatly and replaced them where she had found them. Although she did not remember them, she felt that a piece of her life that she had forever lost was regained, taking another long look at the items then she turned to Tammy.

"May I take the blanket?" Elizabeth requested softly.

"Of course, you may, dear girl," Tammy enfolded her in her arms and Elizabeth experienced a feeling of familiarity. "Everything that you see in here is yours, so you may take whatever you choose to, Lizzy."

Elizabeth picked up the blanket with reverence. On the return to the drawing room, Elizabeth asked her maid to place the blanket on her pillows. From that night on, she would sleep with a little piece of her pervious life at Longbourn with her.

~~~~~~~/~~~~~~~
~~~~~~~

The Lucases, Longs, and Gouldings had dinner at Longmeadow the evening that the Bingleys and Bennets arrived home. They would all be to Netherfield Park on the morrow, but they did not want to descend on the mourning family the same day that they arrived home.

As much as they wanted to condole with their friends to support, they also could not wait to see Lady Elizabeth Fitzwilliam. "I have a feeling that she will be at Netherfield on the morrow," Cheryl Long opined. "She has known the Bingleys for a number of years."

"It is capital that Bennet has been reunited with his Lizzy," Sir William added in his affable manner.

"From what Tammy wrote, he did not exert his rights to demand that she return to live at Longbourn nor does he intend to, and I, for one, applaud that decision," Lady Lucas shared.

"The Fitzwilliams are the only family she has known. She was but one when that insane Fanny had her taken!" Jenny Goulding added stridently.

"Just remember not to mention that woman's name in front of any of the Bennets or their family," Spencer Goulding reminded his wife.

"You are correct husband. That person does not deserve her name mentioned by any of us, I apologise to all for my slip," answered Mrs Goulding contritely.

"Her ladyship is older than I am is she not?" asked Mandy who was fourteen.

"I believe that she will soon be sixteen, Mandy," Cheryl informed her daughter. Both had been shining lights in her life since their parents were tragically murdered in France some eight years earlier. Cara, like Mariah Lucas with whom she was best of friends, was twelve.

"Do you think that she will treat us as if we are socially below her?" Cara asked softly.

"From what Tammy has described as Lady Elizabeth's character I do not believe so," Lady Lucas smiled gently at the girl. "Add to that what the Bingleys have said of her over the years, I imagine she is a little like Jane, very pleasant as long as you do not anger her."

"Our Janey is going to be a Duchess!" Mandy added dreamily.

"Yes, that good news was almost lost in the revelation of finding Elizabeth and poor Mr Bingley's death," Jenny Goulding pointed out.

"Will the Bingleys be able to attend her wedding?" Mandy asked.

"Attending the church ceremony will be perfectly acceptable, but they will not attend the wedding breakfast." Her mother explained.

Franklin Lucas was sitting off in the corner scheming. He had lost his prize; for that is how he saw Jane and her dowry, and exactly the cause of why she would have never accepted him. Now, however, there was another Bennet daughter—not only rich, but rich and titled too. Yes, he deserved such a wife. He knew that she was not yet sixteen, but as far as he was concerned, she was old enough—even if he had to compromise her.

~~~~~~~~/~~~~~~~~

On turning off the road toward Netherfield, the black banner on the gatepost was flapping in the breeze as the convoy from Longbourn made its way to the house. The doors were adorned with black wreathes, and all male servants wore black armbands. When the estate was sold, the servants were given the option to remain with the Bingleys or take a post at one of the Bennet estates, and in a singular voice, every single one had elected to stay as Bingley employees. Once a certain daughter—who was nevermore mentioned—had left the house, it had been as pleasant as could be working for the Bingleys.

The ladies had come without the men, except of course Biggs, Johns, four footmen guards, and four outriders. With the exceptions of Georgiana and Kitty, all of the women residing at Longbourn had come, and Charlotte Pierce had accompanied them for the journey. Elizabeth liked the older woman instantly, and it seemed the admiration was mutual so by the time they arrived at their destination they were using each other's familiar
~~~~~~~~

name, though for some reason Charlotte called Elizabeth 'Eliza', to which she did not object. It felt exactly right when Mrs Pierce used that appellation. Jane, Charlotte, and Elizabeth went to the parlour where Louisa was sitting with her daughter, Mary.

The rest of the ladies were shown into the drawing room where they joined ladies from the neighbourhood who had come to express their sympathies. The only three neighbourhood ladies who knew the true connection to Lady Elizabeth had honoured the request to not share the information. They were disappointed that the very lady in question did not join them but understood that she, Jane, and Charlotte were sitting with Mrs Hurst as they were friends of long-standing.

William had ridden to Netherfield earlier to be with Charles and they were in the study, going over records. "I am his sole heir, Darcy," Bingley frowned as he stared at the copy of his father's will he had removed from the safe. "How am I to do this? I know what I do *not* know, and I currently do *not know anything* about managing an estate."

"Well then you are in luck, my friend, because I do," Will told him. It was not a boast, just the truth. "My father has been training me since I was out of leading strings, and not only that but Uncle Bennet is your neighbour who, until your father purchased Netherfield, successfully managed this and two larger estates!"

"I know that you know how, how does it help me learn how to do this in a few days' time? It is impossible for anyone, except possibly Lizzy to learn all of it so fast." Charles smiled thinly when Will guffawed.

"On the supposition that you would need some help, I have permission from my father to stay for as long as you need me after the funeral. I will teach you like my father taught me," Will stated with a grin.

"As long as you *teach* me and not just do it. In the past, I have deferred to you and others, and I know that is not the way one should live their life. If I am to learn, I must make the decisions. Advice will be good and appreciated, as would helping me see more options or parts of something difficult, but not more than that," Charles insisted.

"That is the only way you will learn, my friend," Will agreed.

Just as tea was being served, the four ladies left the parlour and entered the drawing room. The three ladies who knew who Elizabeth was, had to fight to keep from rushing her to hug her and proclaim to all who she was. They and the rest of the ladies thought that Jane Bennet was the prettiest young lady that they had ever seen, until the raven-haired beauty with her shining hazel eyes with the flecks of green and gold walked into the room.

Elaine then introduced her daughter to the ladies. Some of them remarked how similar her colouring was to that of young Kitty Bennet except for the eyes, for Kitty had her mother's eyes. The ladies had been talking and condoling for a while when the men arrived, and with them came Franklin Lucas.

He congratulated himself on his choice once he saw the most beautiful woman that his eyes had ever beheld. He watched her subtlety, or at least he thought that he was being subtle. Four men took note of his inappropriate interest in Elizabeth, four men who one did not want to run afoul of, and a fifth, more dangerous than the others would be arriving in a few days. It was not only her relatives that noticed the interest from the Lucas heir, but Elizabeth herself.

She felt a chill run down her spine and moved to be as far away from the man as possible. He would have made a move to get closer to her, but she sat between Andrew and Will. When Franklin looked at his chosen target again, he was met by a stare from Will Darcy that left him no doubt that his interest had been detected, and was not welcome. He noticed too that the Earl was looking at him in the same way, as was Mr Bennet and the man he now knew was Mr Darcy. He turned away, deciding that he would have to be a lot more careful until he had affected the compromise.

When Sir William was preparing to depart, he was asked to join Bennet in Bingley's study. When he entered, he was met by not only Bennet, but Mr Darcy, his heir, and the Earl of Matlock. "How may I be of service?" the ebullient man asked.

"Lucas, I hate to raise this with you but all of us here," Bennet indicated the three men standing with him, "noticed Franklin paying Lady Elizabeth a lot of inappropriate attention, so much so that it made her feel very uncomfortable."

"Franklin is a good boy, he would never harm Lady Elizabeth or anyone else," Sir William defended his heir.

"Be that as it may," Andrew said, "my sister is not yet out and will not be for another two years. Please make sure that your son knows that he is to keep his distance from her."

"Bennet, she is your daughter, you know my son would never..." he started, but Bennet cut him off.

"I would hope that too, Lucas, but I saw the way that your son was leering at Elizabeth today. The Earl here is her legal guardian, but were he not, I would be asking you the same thing. If Franklin has no intentions toward her then he will have no objection to maintaining his distance," Bennet stated reasonably.

"I will talk to him," the now sullen man acquiesced, gave a curt bow, and left the office.

"In all of the years I have known him, I have never seen him vexed before," Bennet told the others.

"When she walks or rides, I will make sure that Aggie is always with her and that Biggs and Johns are aware of this potential threat," Andrew stated.

"Good," Will added, "the father may not want to believe it, but I know what I saw and there was nothing benevolent in that man's assessment of our Lizzy."

"I hope that he has more good sense than that, son," George vocalised what they were all hoping.

~~~~~~~/~~~~~~~

When they got back to Lucas Lodge, Sir William summoned his oldest. "Sit, Franklin," he commanded. "Why were you watching Lady Elizabeth at Netherfield, so much so that it was noted by a number of her relatives."

"I-it was so many years since she had been taken, I just was
~~~~~~~

fascinated thinking of how it came about that she was reunited with her father and his family," he lied as smoothly as he could.

"That confirms what I told her brother and the others before I left Netherfield." Sir William needed to believe his son. He, too, had seen behaviours since Jane Bennet had rejected his son that had bothered him, but he ignored them and hoped for the best.

"The Earl spoke to you about me, father?" Franklin asked angrily. His father did not know that he held a grudge against members of the Ton for the treatment he had suffered from some at Oxford, due to his ties to trade and that his father, although a knight, was poor.

"Yes, the Earl, Bennet, and the two Darcy men." He proceeded to relay the gist of the conversation. Once he had related all he added, "As I am sure that you are an honourable man and have no intentions towards a young lady not yet out, it should be no hardship for you to keep your distance from Lady Elizabeth."

"No trouble at all," Franklin prevaricated. He schooled his countenance and left the study, but once in his chambers, he gave vent to his fury. "They will see," he told the wall that he had just hit, "she will be mine!"

CHAPTER 7

Richard arrived at Longbourn on the morning of the nine and twentieth of November, a Tuesday. He was welcomed warmly by all, especially James, Tom, and Alex who were interested in all things soldier. After he changed out of his regimentals, they were not as happy to see him. It was not like he had tales of battles to report, as he was still training men who would be sent forward in some future conflict.

As Franklin Lucas had kept away from Elizabeth, it was decided not to say anything to Richard unless he asked as his family was very aware that he would not take kindly to the man's attention to his youngest sister. They did not want Richard doing something that he would regret later if he gave into his anger over a perceived breach no one would consider as such unless forewarned.

What no one realised or could have guessed was that the only reason they had not seen the Lucas heir was that he was hidden in the woods near Longbourn waiting for his chance to take what he was owed. His anger had grown in proportion with his frustration as his 'intended' had only been seen in public venues with persons surrounding her at all times. After another day of fruitless watching, he decided it was time to cause some trouble. It may not get him nearer to the object of his desire, but it would make him feel a little better.

That evening he took himself to the bar at the Royal Crown Inn. He bought a round of drinks for some of the men who he knew could be counted on to spread gossip prolifically. He did not take into consideration that the rumours would be easily traced back to him as he was too bent on causing pain to think logically.

"You know that Lady Elizabeth, the supposed cousin of the Bennets," he hedged conspiratorially.

"What do you mean 'supposed cousin'?" a man whose wife was the biggest gossip in Meryton challenged.

Franklin leaned in, indicating that the men should huddle in a pretence of not wanting to speak too loudly. "I heard that she is the long-lost Bennet daughter, but those toffs refuse to return her to her rightful father!" He did not lower the volume of his voice so was heard by a good number of the patrons, among them Frank Phillips, who was sharing a drink with a good friend of his. Frank excused himself, went home, and had his horse saddled, heading for Longbourn with all speed.

~~~~~~~/~~~~~~~

Just before they were to sit down for the midday meal, Nichols notified the master that a number of carriages had been seen in the drive. The contingent from Scarborough had arrived in time to pay their respects to the late Oscar Bingley.

Before anyone was assigned chambers, Martha and her two children found themselves being enfolded in a supportive hug after supportive hug, as all family members on both sides had arrived. Martha, who had been strong for days since her husband passed, sobbed in her mother's arms while her siblings encircled them with love.

It did not take Charles long to see that there were too many for Netherfield to accommodate, so he excused himself and wrote a note to his neighbour to ascertain whether Bennington Fields was still available. The groom returned with an affirmative answer, and not long after the Bennets, Darcys, and Fitzwilliam joined the large party at Netherfield.

Once it was decided who would stay where, William and John guided out the three families that would reside at Bennington Fields for the next sennight. Charles Bingley was most appreciative of the assist from Mr Bennet, as it would have been uncomfortably crowded at Netherfield without it.

When the families who would be hosted at the Fields arrived, they were met by Mrs Tess Kennedy, the housekeeper who had
~~~~~~~

received notice from her master to expect the group. Chambers were assigned upon surveying the families, and once everyone had washed and changed, the two Bennet sons accompanied them back to Netherfield.

~~~~~~~~/~~~~~~~

A group had just returned to Longbourn from their visit to assist the Bingleys and found an irate Frank Phillips waiting for their return. He requested to immediately speak to his brother Bennet with the added suggestion that the Fitzwilliam, Darcy men, and his Grace, who had arrived that morning with his mother, be included in their discussion.

The door had barely closed before Phillips stated the reason for his request. "When I was at the Royal Crown with Peter Cromwell, I had the displeasure of hearing that no good Lucas trying to cause trouble for us," Phillips spat out in disgust.

"What was he saying?" Andrew drew up to his full height, keeping himself in check until the facts were shared. As Phillips recounted what he heard, the anger built among the men in the room.

"Why would he do such a thing?" Richard demanded.

"I think that I may have an idea," Perry volunteered. "He imagined himself a viable suitor for Jane while she did not—even before we declared for one another. At her coming-out ball, he claimed that everything was settled, and that he had no hard feelings, but it seems he may have prevaricated."

"We did not want to mention this to you, Richard," Andrew said carefully, "but the first time that this man saw Lizzy at Netherfield, his attention was too marked to be appropriate. We did not think it was an issue any longer as we spoke to his father and asked him to warn his son off. Until today, we had seen neither hide nor a hair of him."

"Now do you think that it is an issue?" Richard asked acerbically. "Where does the Lucas family live?"

"On our Western border," Bennet informed him. Before anyone could say a word, Richard wheeled and marched out of the study, calling for his horse, and the rest of the men followed
~~~~~~~~

closely behind him.

"Richard!" Andrew tried to gain his brother's attention, aware of his own anger, and knew his brother had a blind rage building. Richard took the role of the protector for all of his sisters most seriously and when he turned to look at Andrew, his face was stone-cold. "Brother, if you end up in gaol or worse, you will be of no help to Lizzy, and, you know that she will blame herself." Andrew played the only trump card he knew would bring his younger brother out of his rage.

"I will restrain myself enough to avoid running afoul of the law," Richard agreed, forcing himself to regulate with a control that awed even those that had never seen it. In less than fifteen minutes the riders arrived at Lucas Lodge and were met by a proud Sir William, who felt the compliment of so many high-born men visiting his humble abode. He was introduced to the new arrival, a lieutenant-colonel and brother to the Earl, who looked resolute and unhappy.

"Lucas, where is your son?" Bennet asked sharply, ignoring his friend's invitation to enter the house.

"He is away from home...oh, here he comes now," Sir William pointed, and all the men turned to see Franklin Lucas ride up to the group looking very smug.

He dismounted and strutted toward them, and before he could open his mouth, a man he had not yet met planted his fist into his face, wiping the smug look off in an instant. Both the Lucas heir and two of his teeth were lying on the ground.

"I do not care who you are, but how dare you come to my house and accost my son in such a fashion!" Sir William bellowed. It was very rare to see him angry, but he had never before seen such violence, and without a cause.

"Although I may have tried a different way, your son deserved that and more, Lucas," Bennet told the spluttering man.

"Why do you say that, Bennet?" the still irate man demanded, his anger only increasing as no reason he could ascertain was cause enough for that.

"I was at the Royal Crown earlier," Phillips stepped forward, "and your heir was starting a rumour about my niece being Bennet's daughter and that the 'toffs', as he called the Fitzwilliams, were refusing to return his Elizabeth to him."

Sir William deflated. He had known Frank Phillips for many years, and one thing he had never known his friend to do was to lie. "I should have taken what you told me more serious, I spoke to him, but I did not check his behaviour. I suppose I did not want to believe that my son would behave so."

As he spoke, Franklin came around. He stood unsteadily and tried to wipe the blood from his mouth and chin, then he felt that his two front teeth were gone. "Bloody hell, what was that for?" he whined.

"Were you at the Royal Crown drinking earlier, Franklin?" his father demanded.

"I may have passed through the inn on my way home, father. Why?" He hedged, certain there was no way that the rumours he planted would have reached the ears of these men as yet, so he decided that dishonesty was the best way out of this, although that meant he still didn't know why he had been attacked and his father was not reprimanding his attacker rather than asking him questions.

"Have you mentioned Lady Elizabeth's true relationship with the Bennet's to anyone?" was his father's next question. Franklin started to worry, but he was sure there was no way that it could be traced back to him.

"No, I have not," he replied confidently, knowing that he was safe because someone else must have said it first and that left him fully in the clear.

"When did you learn to lie so easily, Franklin?" asked his disappointed father.

"Father, I am not..." He managed no more because Mr Phillips stepped forward.

"I was in the bar, and I heard every *word* that you said!" Phillips stated clearly.

"Where are my manners," Andrew said sarcastically, "let me introduce our pugilist to you, this is my brother; the Honourable

Lieutenant-Colonel Richard Fitzwilliam, who, like the rest of us, will do *anything* to protect Lady Elizabeth."

"Why, Franklin, why would you do this to our best friends in the neighbourhood?" Sir William asked plaintively.

"Because the toffs all deserve it after what the likes of you did to me at Oxford! Jane was supposed to be mine, and this one," he pointed at Perry malevolently, "steals her from me, so I decided that the sister would do. I cannot help it if the little doxy is yet…" Whatever he was about to say was stopped as both Will and Richard hit him with all of their force in his midsection, the blows connecting at the same instant as if intended and Franklin fell to his knees gasping for air.

Richard lifted his head by his hair so that the spluttering man would be able to see his eyes. "If you ever so much as look in my sister's direction again, I will call you out, and I promise you that will be the last mistake you *ever* make! Do I make myself clear?" Franklin nodded his head while still gasping for air.

"Whatever happened to you at Oxford was not right, Franklin, but neither is your blaming nor disdaining anyone who is highborn because of it. My daughter had never done anything to offend you, so direct your venom at the ones that wronged you, not at innocents. What you did in retaliation is the way that a coward would react. Is it not much easier to hurt an innocent while hiding behind a rumour than face the ones who actually wronged you?" Bennet stated. "Lucas, I trust that you will take care of this."

"You have my word, Bennet," a much-saddened Sir William promised. Lady Sarah Lucas had been standing in the doorway after shooing her younger daughter and son back into the house. She had felt that something was not quite right with her oldest son, but she never suspected he was this deep into his delusions. She hoped that his actions would not cause her to be shunned in the neighbourhood.

Frank's first reaction was to scoff at Mr Bennet's words, but then, as his breathing slowly returned to normal and with the pain from his mouth and stomach as a vivid reminder, Franklin

Lucas felt shame like he had never felt before. "Mr Bennet has the right of it; I acted as a coward does. I will not bother any of you again; you have my word on that. I will go back to the inn as I am now and tell the men that I was talking out of turn and what I said was all untrue," he offered in contrition.

"As much as I appreciate your willingness to attempt a repair of what you have wrought, I believe that we will not be able to put the cat back into the bag. We will have to decide on the best way forward," Bennet stated thoughtfully. "Gentlemen, let us to Longbourn to consider how to handle this, unless either you or the Colonel have an objection, your grace." Bennet looked at both Fitzwilliam men. The men standing with Bennet nodded in agreement and started to mount their horses. "Lucas, know that I do not hold you and the rest of your family responsible for your son's actions, and I hope that his words here were not just words, but that he is sincere in his desire to correct his behaviour."

"I swear on my life, Mr Bennet, I am," Franklin stated unequivocally.

"If not, it *will* be your life," Richard murmured loud enough that those around him could hear, and all knew he was not joking. Bennet mounted after shaking his friend's hand to reinforce his words of not blaming him, and the men headed down the drive back to Longbourn.

When they arrived at their destination, Andrew pulled Bennet aside. "We need to have a family meeting that includes *all* who will be affected. I can tell you that my sister will not react well if we make a decision behind closed doors without including her, as it affects her more than any of us," Andrew told his new uncle.

"Then a family meeting it will be," Bennet resolved. He was sorry that a matter of business had called his brother Gardiner and his family back to town a few days earlier, but he expected the Gardiners to return before the funeral service the next day. Gardiner was a very intelligent man, and Bennet would have enjoyed his and his wife's perspectives on the way forward.

~~~~~~~/~~~~~~~
~~~~~~~

"Franklin, do you realise that you could have ruined us all if Bennet had not been so benevolent?" Sir William demanded once he, his heir, and wife were in his study with the door shut. "Charlotte is well married, but do you have any idea what you would have caused for Mariah and John?"

For the first time in many years, Franklin Lucas wept openly, and his mother hugged him. "I am so sorry and ashamed of my actions," he repeated until he calmed down.

"We are sorry that you had to endure what you did at Oxford. Why did you not tell us?" Sarah Lucas asked.

"I felt that as a man I had to find a solution on my own. I know now that I should have sought your counsel, seeing how terribly I have behaved. In my mind, I held all of the first circles responsible for the handful at Oxford who tormented me. I knew that Jane Bennet had a large dowry, and with it I would no longer be poor, I would be accepted, and when she accepted the Duke just after rejecting me, something in me snapped. It was only today, when I literally had the sense knocked into me, that I woke up to what I have been doing and planning. I am deeply ashamed of myself and horrified at my own actions." His parents glanced at one another and neither doubted that Franklin was contrite and had seen the error of his ways.

"The mark of a true man, my son, is not that he never makes a mistake, but how he goes about fixing his mistakes and taking the responsibility for them. We will wait to hear from Longbourn regarding their decisions, and then we will help in any way that they see fit," Sir William stated resolutely, and his wife and son agreed without reservation.

~~~~~~~~/~~~~~~~~

After dinner, all of the family except for the youngest members in the nursery met in Longbourn's largest drawing room. Mr Hill was instructed that they were not to be disturbed, and after the door was closed Andrew and Bennet informed those who did not know of what Franklin Lucas had done and the confrontation at Lucas Lodge.

"What will we do, Andrew? I thought that I had more time
~~~~~~~~

before the world knew of my true connection to my birth family," Elizabeth asked.

"As did we all, Sprite," Andrew responded sympathetically.

"We do not have to decide today, and Mr Bingley's funeral is on the morrow. If you want to think about this and what you prefer, Lizzy, we can revisit the topic after we return from Netherfield," Bennet offered.

Elizabeth took a moment to consider the new situation. "No, Uncle Thomas, there is no need to wait. The reason I waited to reveal my true connection was allow me time to know my birth family without the scrutiny of others, especially the Ton. It seems that young Mr Lucas has taken that decision out of our hands. I do not see another option. We need to announce the truth before the rumours take hold," Elizabeth proposed.

"We could try and contain the news to Meryton and its environs," Frank Phillips suggested.

"Given how much interest there is in Lizzy, I am sure that the rumours will be sold or leaked to a London gossip rag," Jane opined the practicality, despite the distastefulness of the possibility.

"My betrothed is correct," Perry added in support of his love, "I do not believe that we can bury this here and hope it does not spread."

"Then we will send a notice to the Times," Andrew resigned himself to the prospect of the Ton's reaction.

"I have a suggestion," Lady Rose spoke for the first time. All eyes turned to her. "Allow me to write to my cousin and have her and the family make a royal announcement. That way no one will be able to question that there is not full support of the families, and make everyone aware that any who try to use the news against us would be rendered mute."

"My mother's plan has merit," Perry agreed.

"What about in Meryton?" William Bennet asked, "not only did Franklin state the true connection, but he also lied about why Lizzy is not living here."

"My Hattie will make sure that the truth is well known,"

Frank Phillips waved that off as it would take but a moment to correct.

"Let us see if he was sincere," Will had a thought. "Lucas said he was willing to tell everyone the truth, so as soon as we announce that the Bennets are in fact Lizzy's birth family, let him tell one and all that he lied about her being forced to live as a Fitzwilliam."

"My son has a good suggestion," Anne Darcy agreed.

"He had better do whatever he can to fix what he broke," Richard bit out, "or I can go *speak* to him again."

"I do not believe that will be needed, Richard," Bennet said with a grin as he visualised Franklin Lucas prostrate on his back. "I believe that his contrition was sincere."

"It will not only be Hattie," Tammy Bennet stated emphatically. "The rest of us, and our friends who know the truth, and I am sure that Sarah Lucas will be very vocal as well. We will all make sure that the truth is known, so if anyone repeats the nonsense about why Lizzy is not with us, they will be looked at with all the ridicule a liar deserves."

With the decisions made, Lady Rose sat and wrote her note to the Queen, and as soon as she finished a Bennet courier was sent racing toward London, to Buckingham House.

"Jane's wedding is in January and all of you are invited, why not stay and spend Christmastide with us?" Tammy suggested. "It will allow us all to get to know one another much better away from the scrutiny of the Ton in London." After brief discussions, all three visiting families accepted the invitation with pleasure.

"Are you well with all of this, Lizzy?" Georgiana asked quietly as she sat next to her best friend and cousin.

"I am, Gigi. We always planned to make the true connection known, it is just a little sooner than I expected. But as we will be away from Town until January, I hope that by then something new will fix the Ton's attention." She squeezed Gigi's hand and nodded that she truly did agree that this was the right course forward.

~~~~~~~/~~~~~~~
~~~~~~~

The day of the funeral was bitingly cold, and the night before there had been a light dusting of snow; which was very early for Hertfordshire. Mr Pierce's service was brief at St Alfred's, the church packed to full capacity with the visiting and local men. After the final prayer of the service, Oscar Bingley's body was moved for the last time, and he was lowered into the grave where he would slumber for eternity.

The Gardiners had arrived barely an hour before the funeral. He would have hated to miss the service as Oscar Bingley had become much more than a partner in business, he was a friend who Edward would miss. Now was not the time to discuss the future of their business ventures, but at some point, he would need to talk to Oscar's brother Paul Bingley about their future endeavours.

Franklin Lucas gave his condolences to Charles Bingley and his family then excused himself. He would keep his word and refused to make Lady Elizabeth or any of her family uneasy with his presence at Netherfield. The men all climbed into the waiting carriages and made their way to the Bingley estate where the women were awaiting them.

Martha was most thankful to be surrounded by all of the support that she had. In addition to her friends from the neighbourhood, her mother, sisters, and sister-in-law were very attentive to her needs. As Martha sat with her mother next to her, she was very pleased that she had insisted that her surviving parent, now seventy, come live with her rather than alone in the house where she had grown up.

Her siblings had supported Martha in her request and had promised to visit as much as possible. As they pointed out to her, they had her company in Scarborough for many years, so they could not begrudge Martha wanting their mother with her and had expected the request to come.

Some three hours after the service and internment, it was just family who remained at Netherfield, and they sat around in groups discussing the lost Bingley patriarch. Before the group residing at Bennington Fields departed, Charles announced that the solicitor would be at Netherfield on the coming Monday to read his father's last will and testament.

CHAPTER 8

To counteract the lie Franklin Lucas had started, the truth of who Lady Elizabeth Fitzwilliam had been born to, was announced at the end of the church services at both Longbourn's church and St. Alfred in Meryton. The ladies who knew the truth immediately went to work to countermand the intimation of why Lady Elizabeth would not be returning to live with her birth family.

Franklin Lucas made sure that he told every man he had talked to at the Royal Crown Inn the night of his attempted revenge that he had not been honest about the reason she was not with the Bennets. A number of the men he had lied to would have liked to hit Franklin, but after seeing the bruises on his face and the missing teeth, they surmised that he had already paid the price for his misdeeds. Once the true reason was widely known, it squelched any repeating of the lie, and there were none who did not understand that Mr Bennet had put his daughter's welfare and needs ahead of his own in making the hard decision.

When it was disclosed how many times the two families had been close to one another without meeting face to face before the connection was discovered, the citizens of Meryton were astonished. They were further astounded when they learned that Mr Bennet had been regularly playing and losing chess matches by mail with his lost daughter for almost two years. One person was heard to say that someone should write a novel about all of the happenings, but it would be so unbelievable that it would have to be considered a work of fiction.

It was at this point that Mr Pierce and his wife were entertaining guests who had been with them for a sennight. Mr

George Austen, his wife Cassandra, and one of their daughters. Austen was a fellow clergyman and had been a friend of Longbourn's rector for many years. Mr Austen held a living in Steveton, Hampshire. Miss Jane Austen felt a kinship to Lady Elizabeth when she found out the young lady was given free and unfettered access to read and study what she wished, like Miss Austen's own father allowed herself. She had just started writing, and as was her wont she took note of some of the names of the people she met in her notebook, which was her constant companion. For some reason, the people felt easy talking to her, and when she was seen taking notes many laughed as they agreed she could use them in her literature at some point. The Austens departed Monday morning as Mr Austen was required back at his parish.

On Monday morning, the fifth of December, there was a full-page royal announcement that informed all that the birth family of Lady Elizabeth Fitzwilliam had been found. The Bennets of Longbourn, who, the information listed, had been on their land for many generations and were members of the first circles in their own right. The only mention of Lady Elizabeth's birth mother was that she had died in childbirth not long after her daughter had been taken from the family.

In a related article, it was revealed that the late Earl of Matlock's murderer, one Sam Hodges, was in fact the kidnapper. It was reported that he had thought his victim was dead until he discovered that she was alive and that the murder of the late Earl was part of a second kidnapping plot which had gone bad thanks to the intervention of Colonel Richard Fitzwilliam. The article went onto say that the reporter had received confirmation from both families that Lady Elizabeth would remain a Fitzwilliam as they were the family that she had grown up with but that she was in connection with the Bennets and both families were glad the decade-plus mystery had culminated in such a conclusion.

With the combination of the royal announcement and the article, sympathy for the Fitzwilliams, the Bennets, and especially Lady Elizabeth, soared. As this was not the first time that the

Bennets had been mentioned with favour by the Royals, members of the Ton were practically salivating for a chance to make a connection with the family. All who were readying themselves for the families to be in Town for the rest of the Little Season or the Season next year were; in the end, destined to be disappointed.

~~~~~~~~/~~~~~~~~

Mr Lloyd Wrightfield, the late Mr Bingley's solicitor, arrived at Netherfield promptly at the time he said he would. The solicitor read the will in such a dry monotone it threatened to put some to sleep. There were no surprises, as Charles had previously discovered a copy of his father's will in his father's safe. At the end, Mr Wrightfield had one codicil that was not in the copy that Charles had read. His father had left the untouched dowry that would have been Caroline's to Louisa. As he had turned the money over to Gardiners and Associates to invest for him, there was a little over twenty thousand pounds in the fund.

After a brief word with Harold, Louisa announced that the money would be used as Mary's dowry, and the decision was roundly praised by the family members present. Once the lawyer's duty had been discharged, he took his leave. When the family started to disperse, Charles quietly asked his Uncle Paul to hold back. "What say you, we send a note to Mr Gardiner to meet on the morrow in the morning to discuss our partnership going forward?" Charles proposed.

"That meets my approval," his Uncle Paul replied. "Will you take a more active role as your father did?"

"I think that I will. My intention is to try to follow in my father's footsteps at the works near Tattersalls. He was happy and proud that that particular location now accounts for almost half of the orders from all three of our branches, so I will be running the estate as well as giving time to the business," Charles agreed. Paul Bingley grinned, truly proud of the man that his nephew had become.

"Have you learnt all you need to about running an estate yet?" Paul Bingley asked his nephew, concerned that he might be tak-
~~~~~~~~

ing on more than he was able to deal with.

"No, I myself know little about estate management, however my friend Darcy has his parent's permission to remain here and teach me. His father has been training him since he was a lad, and in the last few years he has taken over the running of their satellite estates. The largest of them, Riverdale in Shropshire, is about the same size as Netherfield, so I feel confident that I will learn much from him," Bingley reassured his uncle.

"That makes me rest easier, knowing that you have his assistance. I did not want you to be overwhelmed by all of your new responsibilities as head of your branch of the Bingley family. Your father would have been proud of you, Charles, as am I." His Uncle Paul's approbation meant much to the nephew.

~~~~~~~/~~~~~~~

"How long will you be away, Will?" Alex asked.

"I am not sure, Alex; it depends on how long it takes me to teach my friend," Will responded, as he tousled his younger brother's sandy blonde hair.

"Is there no one else that can teach him?" Georgiana wanted to know.

"If you are here, how will we debate?" Elizabeth asked anxiously. She knew full well that was not the only reason that she did not want to be parted from her cousin.

"Firstly, you will be here until after your sister's, I mean your cousin's, wedding, then your birth family will travel north with the rest of you for a month. Mayhap you will be too busy showing everyone around Snowhaven and Pemberley to even notice my absence!" Will pointed out.

"I forgot that James and Tom will be visiting us!" an excited Alex exclaimed. Forgotten was his pique at his older brother staying in Hertfordshire, as it was replaced with the desire to find his cousins and make plans for their visit.

"It will be hard without my big brother to protect me!" Georgiana teased as she stuck her lip out in an exaggerated fake pout.

"Do not make me tickle you, Georgie," Will threatened with a big grin.
~~~~~~~

“Anything, but that!” the extremely ticklish girl gasped, deciding that it was time to withdraw before her brother made good on his threat.

Mrs Annesley smiled as she watched Lady Elizabeth and her cousin William from the corner. Even if the two would not, or more correctly, could not admit that they had tender feelings for each other, it was rather obvious to her.

“We can play chess by post like I did with my birth father,” Elizabeth suggested.

“Mayhap, we will have to see. I wonder if it will feel better losing to you when you are not sitting opposite me,” Will teased, pride swelling his chest as his cousin giggled. Will knew that the hardest part of being away would be not seeing the young woman sitting opposite him. He was confident, however, that with the relationship between her and the Bennets in the open, that there would be a good amount of opportunity to see her during his time advising and teaching his friend.

Though true both had tender feelings for the other, neither knew the other did and as Elizabeth was not yet out, it was not a subject that either would canvass.

~~~~~~~~/~~~~~~~~

Edward Gardiner arrived at Netherfield at the appointed time and Nichols showed him into the master’s study where Charles and Paul Bingley stood to welcome him. Charles asked Nichols to bring them coffee and some pastries. Once they had consumed the refreshments, their discussion of business commenced.

Charles was assured that his Uncle Paul and Mr Gardiner would be willing to help him when he requested it, but that unless they saw a substantial error about to be made, they did not intend to offer unsolicited advice. Gardiner reported on Gardiner and Associates’ earnings for the previous quarter, and that the business was on track to meet or even exceed the previous year’s performance.

Paul Bingley reported that all indications were that the three Bingley Carriage works operations would beat the fifteen thousand pounds in profits that they had made the previous year. He
~~~~~~~~

recommended that they follow what his late brother had put in place—that twenty percent of the profits be reinvested.

For Charles Bingley, it meant that his profits from the business plus that of the estate would give him between seven and eight thousand pounds per annum. He did not need more than that, so he too saw the sense of the percentage that went to investments being allowed to continue as it had been.

When Gardiner asked about the estate, the younger Bingley told him about Darcy's offer. Edward agreed that it was wise to ask for help when needed, and from what he could tell, the Darcy heir was an extremely competent young man. Gardiner relayed his brother Bennet's offer of help whenever it was needed, in case either of them preferred to ask a third opinion.

After business was completed, the three discussed how each of them missed the late Oscar Bingley, and although it was early yet, they raised a snifter of brandy to toast the man they knew and loved.

~~~~~~~~/~~~~~~~

A few days later, when the London papers reached Packwood, there was an eruption of epic proportions. "This is not to be borne!" Mrs Fitzpatrick ranted. "She is not the daughter of a servant! How can this be? I said that she was, and I know it must be so! They are all lying!"

"Are you well, Mrs Fitzpatrick," George Wickham asked. At one and twenty, his life was the same, an indentured servant to the delusional woman, but until he found a way to get her money, he would have to play along. He would need the money to exact his revenge.

"Read that!" she pointed a bony finger at the newspapers that she had flung on the floor in disgust. The more Wickham read, the more infuriated he became, though he had to school his countenance in front of the old lady. The mongrel was not a mongrel! Not only was she living the life that he believed belonged to him, but she was the daughter of a wealthy landowner. Then he saw it.

"Hodges was the one that kidnapped her!" he exclaimed.
~~~~~~~~

"Yes, and he had the gall not to tell me. It was my right to know all of his closest concerns, and more assuredly any information with regards to her! He is lucky that he is already dead! And you, useless boy!" She brought her walking stick down on Wickham's shoulder hard. "You tried to kill her and missed, and all you did was put them on alert! All of these years later and my spies cannot get close to either family. They think they are so clever; well, I am cleverer than all of them," she cackled.

"What do you mean?" Wickham asked as he rolled his shoulder to ease the pain of the blow. He could have reached for her neck with his hands, and had the pleasure of squeezing the life out of her body slowly, but he needed blunt, and she had it, but he just did not know where!

"You will find out when it is time, boy," she answered cryptically. "Then you will be told more, but not before." What the former Lady Catherine de Bourgh was not telling her pet was that she had bribed a man to get work at Pemberley. He was to make no contact for the first year, so he would not engender any suspicion. In the summer of the next year, he was to meet with one of her men for instructions. Then, when her erstwhile family least suspected it, she would strike and avenge herself on them!

~~~~~~~/~~~~~~~

Greg Jones had made the easiest money in his life. The old lady had paid him two hundred pounds, more than he would see in almost ten years, to get hired at Pemberley. When he arrived at the estate a year earlier, they had been looking for men to work in the stables. Jones believed that this would suit his benefactor as she wanted information about their movements; the stables would be a good place from which to hear the family's travel plans.

What Jones did not know is that among the stable staff were five guards who were passed off as working in the stables as he was. Two were assistant drivers, one a groom, and two that did similar work as Jones. As he knew no one in the area being from Warwickshire, he became very close to a fellow stable hand, John
~~~~~~~

Branch. In fact, as far as Jones was concerned, John was his best and only friend. A few months ago, Jones had picked a fight with a man in Kympton. Unfortunately, the man's brothers were close by and were about to issue a beat down until John Branch rescued him and so, in Greg's estimation, saved his life. And John had never asked for anything except his friendship. Jones decided that when the time came, his friend John would be the loyal kind of man that he would be able to confide in, and help him accomplish whatever task the old lady wanted him to do.

~~~~~~~/~~~~~~~

Thanks to the decision to stay at Longbourn until after the wedding, the Darcy and Fitzwilliam ladies' horses were sent for. The next day, after Andrew and George Darcy wrote their missives, three grooms arrived leading Callisto, Saturn, and Brown Beauty. Only Aggie seemed happier than their riders that the three horses arrived. She knew that when she saw her mistress's horse, it meant that long runs were in her future.

She was correct, as a long ride was being planned for the morrow where the guests would be introduced to Oakham Mount. They would all leave early, watch the sunrise, and then ride to a glade between Longbourn and Bennington Fields where the group would have a picnic lunch.

Anne de Bourgh was extremely excited, not because her horse had arrived, but because Ian Ashby had been invited to Longbourn. She had barely begun her formal courtship when they left London. As he was Andrew's friend, she had begged her brother to invite him. Andrew had consulted Marie, and she had pointed out that with so many in the house, and with them having recently moved to the family floor while he would stay on a guest floor, that propriety would be maintained. Much to Anne's delight, after garnering permission from the mistress of the estate, Andrew had sent the invitation to his friend who had accepted. He would be arriving in two days' time.

The group of riders gathered early in the morning as dawn was starting to lighten the sky in the east. All the younger residents, except the twins and Alex, were in the party. The various
~~~~~~~

parents had begged off, preferring to get more sleep. Aggie was jumping up and down in excitement as she loved to run alongside her mistress when she rode. The group was accompanied by grooms and footmen, led, as was usual, by Biggs and Johns.

They set off, exiting the park, heading north through Longbourn's orchards. The four Bennets in the party pointed out various features to their cousins, or in Perry's case, soon to be brother-in-law. They passed the little folly that was a replica of a Greek temple, then entered the forest around the base of Oakham Mount. As they exited the forest, the land started to rise gently until they reached the path that led them up the side of the mount. Oakham Mount was not a mountain, it was simply the only hill of any height in the area, so the view was beautiful.

When they gained the flat crest, they dismounted, the ladies assisted by males in the party. William helped Elizabeth down and felt a fission of pleasure as his hands held her waist. He lowered her to the ground, schooling his features so he would not broadcast his thoughts to all in the party. Had he known that his cousin had felt the same, if not more pleasure at the intimate feel of his touch, it would have pleased him greatly.

There was a large, ancient oak tree on the eastern side of the crest with a big rock next to it which was ideal to act as a bench. Having run circles around them, Aggie flopped down next to the rock and was soon dozing. While the group watched, the first tendrils of the sun's rays started to peek over the horizon in the east. The sky became ablaze with light and colour as the few clouds that there were seemed to glow with a golden hue. For those who had not had the pleasure before, it was a spectacular sight, and the Bennets, who had seen it many times, never grew tired of sharing it.

"It is easy to understand why you recommended this location, Jane," Elizabeth told her older sister as she wound her arm around Jane's.

"That is Longbourn," James proudly pointed out his home to the south. "To the west are Bennington fields. You can see Meryton to the east, and beyond it," he pointed, "is Netherfield Park."

"I pray for the Bingleys each night," William Bennet shared. "They have family around them now to support them, but some will leave today, and within a week it will be just them. At least Mrs Bingley's mother will live with her now."

"They will still have much support, William," Jane pointed out. "They are well-liked in the neighbourhood, and all of their friends will make sure to visit and assist as they get through this most trying of times. Also, do not forget that cousin, Will, will be with them helping Charles learn how to be confident in his role as the master of an estate."

"I could see myself climbing that tree and reading in it for hours," Elizabeth stated as she changed the subject.

"Did we mention that our sister had a penchant to climb trees when she was younger," Andrew informed the smiling group.

"Do not be disingenuous, Andrew," Will called him out with a grin.

"I was not being so, Will," was the response heavy with mock indignation.

"When she was younger? If my information is correct, our *Lady* Elizabeth," he gave his blushing cousin a put-on bow, "still can be found up her favourite tree at Snowhaven occasionally."

"Unlike you, Will, I was trying to be chivalrous and not cause my sister embarrassment!" Andrew returned.

"Are you trying to make up for Itch having to return to London by taking his place in teasing and embarrassing me, Will?" Elizabeth asked pertly, her blush rising as their banter continued, as her heart raced. Will raised his hands in surrender, but the huge grin on his face showed that he was not contrite in the least.

'How I would have loved to have grown up with such a sister!' Jane told herself as the group mounted their horses to ride to the glade where breakfast would be waiting for them. She was happy that Lizzy had been adopted by a family that clearly adored her, but she was sad for the relationship that she had not had over the years with her younger sister.

~~~~~~~/~~~~~~~
~~~~~~~

"Come in, Franklin," Charlotte welcomed her older brother to the parsonage to join them to break their fasts. "Mr Jones did a credible job in replacing some teeth for you, brother, although at the time you deserved worse than that!" Charlotte admonished him.

"I am well aware of how abhorrent my behaviour was, Charlotte. There is no rebuke that you can issue me that I have not already said to myself. I feel tremendous shame when I think on what I was planning to do," Franklin said, his head bowed as they entered the small dining parlour where Mr Pierce awaited the siblings.

"Have you apologised, brother?" Pierce asked pointedly.

"Yes, to Mr Bennet and our parents," he agreed.

"I know that, but have you made your sincere apology to Lady Elizabeth, as she was the real object of your dishonourable plans." Pierce pressed his point.

"No, but I swore that I would not go near her, and her brother in the Royal Dragoons made it perfectly clear that if I approached her, or even looked at her, he would end me."

"My suggestion is *not* that you approach her. Request an audience with the Earl and ask his permission to deliver your apologies to his sister. If he refuses, which he very well might as you deserve, make them to him to pass on to her," Pierce suggested.

"I agree with Christopher," Charlotte stated. "If the Earl allows it, it will be cathartic for her to hear the words from your own mouth. I would suggest that you start with Mr Bennet and canvass his opinion on whether or not the Earl would be willing to receive you yet. If you go after our meal, you will not run into Lady Elizabeth or any of the younger family as they have taken a ride this morning and will not be back before eleven."

And so that was decided. The rector led them in grace, and then the three enjoyed their meal. Franklin was feeling lighter than he had for days with the decision to try to make his apology to the very lady who he had never had cause to harm.

~~~~~~~/~~~~~~~

"It is so pretty here," Elizabeth exclaimed as they arrived at
~~~~~~~

the glade. There was an open grassy area where the servants had two tables set with much food displayed. There were chairs and blankets spread around. To one side was a lazy stream that burbled and bubbled along its way, with tall reeds on the opposite bank, and the croaking of a loud toad.

"It is so nice here, Lizzy," Georgiana enthused. "Should we sit on a blanket?"

"Yes, we shall, Gigi. We should leave the chairs for the much older members of our group," Elizabeth stated impertinently with an arched eyebrow as she looked at the group that included her brother and his wife, Will, and Perry.

"You will pay for that impertinence later, Sprite!" Andrew warned playfully. "For now, I will take a moment to rest these old bones in a chair." He teased her, gaining a laugh from many more than just their Lizzy and a smile from his wife that made him feel like the luckiest man in the world.

While the group was enjoying breaking their fast and communing with one another and nature, Franklin Lucas was being shown into a drawing room at Longbourn where the Bennet and Darcy parents were settled into conversation with Ladies Elaine and Rose. Bennet arched his eyebrow in question when he saw who walked into the room, and when Lady Elaine saw the way Bennet did so, she could not help but smile. '*So that is where my daughter inherited that arching of her eyebrow.*'

"May I speak to you in your study, Mr Bennet?" Franklin requested quietly.

"There is nothing that you could have to say to me that you cannot say in front of everyone here," Bennet returned sharply. He would forgive the Lucas heir openly, but he would not make things easy for him.

"I am seeking your advice on whether it is wise to approach the Earl to request that he allow me to offer my sincere apologies to Lady Elizabeth," Franklin explained, his eyes downcast toward his feet.

"Elaine, you know your son much better than I," Bennet deferred to Elizabeth's mother.

"Andrew will hear you out, young man. Whether or not he will allow you to address his sister, I do not know. I can tell you that if he allows it, it will be before more than just he and her in the room. No matter how contrite you are, or seem to be, you will never be allowed alone with my daughter under *any* circumstances!" Elaine told Franklin acerbically.

"I deserve no less, your Ladyship," Franklin said as he lifted his head so that the people sitting and watching him could see the sincerity in his eyes. "My actions and what I planned were despicable, and I deserved much more than I received from your sons," he looked from the Dowager Countess to the Darcys. "All I can do is to apologise as much as I am allowed and try to live a good and honourable life, never repeating the mistakes of the past."

"As Christians, we place a high value on repentance and forgiveness, as long as the repentance is genuine," Tammy Bennet stated to ease the way for those who had taken the deepest of exception after Frank's actions and there were some nods of agreement in the room, though she knew it would take Elaine and Thomas longer.

"My son will expect you this afternoon, and he will be able to tell if your contrition is genuine or not," Elaine told the young man in dismissal. Frank bowed to all and took his leave. At least he would be able to make his apology to the Earl, even if he was never personally allowed to deliver it to the lady in question.

CHAPTER 9

When Andrew was informed that the man who had tried to hurt his sister wanted to meet with him, his first inclination was to refuse, until Marie had placed a calming hand on his arm as they listened to what those who had spoken to the man earlier had to say. Once he had calmed down and considered it logically, he allowed that he needed to hear the young man out. He would make a decision about him delivering an apology to Lizzy if he decided that the apology was sincere, and *only* if Lizzy agreed to it.

Rather than keep her in the dark, Andrew sought out his sister and asked her to join him in the large drawing room, where all except the youngest three were congregated. Bennet relayed the gist of the conversation that had been held with Franklin Lucas, with her mother and others giving their perspectives as well. When they were done relaying the information, she looked to Andrew.

"It seems that he has seen the error of his ways and is truly repentant. If you make the same judgement after you speak to him then I will listen to what he says, but who will be with me?" Elizabeth asked. Even though it sounded as if he was sincere, she would not feel comfortable having just Mrs Annesley with her if Andrew gave his permission for the apology.

"As many of us as you desire," her mother answered emphatically. "That too is your decision, dearest; we can all be there or some of us, you can let us know." Elizabeth considered her words carefully.

"I would like Andrew, Marie, Mama, Will, Uncle George, Aunt Anne, Anne, Aunt Tammy, and Father Bennet," she imparted. The room went silent at the new appellation for Thomas Bennet, who was holding his breath, hoping that he had not misheard.

"As the true relationship is known, there is no purpose in calling my birth family anything except what they are," Elizabeth informed all matter-of-factly. "Father Bennet is in fact my birth father, and his children are my sisters and brothers. Rather than losing my loving family, I have a larger one than I have only recently gotten to enjoy spending time with."

Jane rose with tears in her eyes and enfolded her sister in a hug similar to the one she did the night that they were reunited. "Since we found you, I have been praying to be able to call you sister and to be called thus in return," Jane said softly in her sister's ear as the hug was returned in full measure. When Jane withdrew, she was replaced by a line of three brothers who all hugged their sister in turn, next was Tammy.

"What am I to call you?" Elizabeth asked softly.

"Aunt Tammy or Tammy will be fine, Lizzy," she answered.

Last was her father, with tears in his eyes as he heard the words that he had dreamed of hearing for nigh on fifteen years. "Please say it again," he asked quietly as he hugged her.

"Father Bennet," she responded just as softly. "I hope you are not disappointed that I am not able to call you Papa, I had the best of men as my papa, and I will never call another such, not even if, and when, I marry one day."

"As I understood that, and I could never tear you from your Fitzwilliam family. I will happily be your 'Father Bennet' going forward," Bennet told his daughter as tears freely streamed down his face.

Once they separated, the twins and Alex were brought down from the nursery as the new status was explained to them. Kitty and Tom were relieved that they did not have to remember to call Lizzy cousin rather than sister.

"I must write to Maddie," Tammy remembered as she wiped her tears of joys from her eyes. "She predicted that this would happen before Lizzy left Longbourn." The Gardiners had returned to London the previous day and would return on the three and twentieth and then remain until after the wedding. "I will also send a note to Hattie; she will be most pleased for us."

The family soon migrated to the large dining parlour for the midday meal as the younger Bennets especially used 'sister' in front of Elizabeth's name as much as possible. Bennet quietly called her daughter a few times, warming the heart of his daughter and himself when he did.

~~~~~~~~/~~~~~~~~

At Netherfield Park the party was reduced to the Hursts, Grandmother Beckett, who could never have enough time with her first great-grandchild, Mary, Paul and Henrietta Bingley, their two younger children, and of course Martha and Charles Bingley.

"I think of my husband all the time and see him everywhere in this house," Martha shared as she blinked back the tears.

"That is but natural when you lose one that you love, daughter," Gwendolyn Beckett comforted her oldest child, "it was like that after your father passed, Martha, although it slowly becomes better, you never stop missing him nor should you try."

"I am so pleased that you have decided to live with me, Mama," Martha kissed her mother's cheek.

"How much longer can you stay with us, Louisa?" Charles asked, "I know that Grandmama Beckett would be happy if you never left, and you know that all three of you are welcome for as long as you desire to stay with us."

"Well, brother, you do have very good brandy and food," Hurst ribbed. "It is up to my lovely wife as we have no fixed engagements for the foreseeable future."

"It would warm my heart to stay with Mama, Charles, and our Grandmother for an extended stay," Louisa responded.

"Then it is settled!" Charles exclaimed. "You will stay as long as you wish."

"If I may, I would like to accompany you and Darcy when he starts teaching you about estate management. It will put me in good stead for one day in the distant future when I inherit Winsdale," Hurst requested.

"There would be no objection from me, brother, and I am
~~~~~~~~

fairly sure that Darcy will not object either. I will put the request to him the next time I see him. He will move to Netherfield after the wedding next month," Charles shared.

"We are very glad that it will not be the two of you in this big house alone," Henrietta Bingley stated. "We will miss all of you, but it will make it somewhat easier to leave you."

"Do not forget our friends from the neighbourhood," Martha reminded her sister-in-law.

"That is true, you have had a steady stream here to support you, especially your five friends from the board that you serve on," Henrietta stated.

"When I am ready, I suppose that I will go back to working with the board and the various projects it has planned. It will keep me busy," Martha said.

The truth was that Martha had been deeply touched at the outpouring of genuine love and sympathy from the neighbourhood, and not just from the families of her five best friends. She knew that it would be hard, and, like her friend Elaine Fitzwilliam, she had decided on two years of mourning for her husband while her children had followed the Fitzwilliam children in choosing to mourn their father for a year.

~~~~~~~/~~~~~~~

As Franklin approached Longbourn he grew nervous, not at the rectitude of his mission but at the way that the Earl would receive him. He could not blame Lord Andrew or any of his family for the way that they had reacted to his request. Now with a full understanding and hindsight, he knew that if anyone had tried to treat his sister in such a way that his reactions would not have been any less than that of Lady Elizabeth's family, including the Lieutenant-Colonel who had cost him two of his teeth. Though truthfully, he was not certain he could be as effective.

He was shown into Mr Bennet's study, where the Earl was seated behind the desk. After a bow, he sat down when his Lordship waved him to do so. "You wanted an interview with me, Mr Lucas. The floor is yours," Andrew said coldly.

"You have my thanks for even agreeing to see me, your Lord-
~~~~~~~

ship. I know that my behaviour was beyond the pale, and no matter my imagined justifications there was nothing that could make what I wanted to do, what I did do, right or proper. I am as disappointed in myself as are my parents and everyone else." Franklin took a deep breath before carrying on. "If you decide that I am not to deliver my apology in person, I will understand and honour your wish to never approach Lady Elizabeth. In fact, if I know that we are to attend the same event, I will absent myself from the said event. In that case, I beseech you to convey my deepest contrition. Neither your sister nor Miss Bennet before her deserved my attentions, which were misguided attempts to right the wrongs from Oxford.

"As Mr Bennet correctly pointed out, I have to confront those who actually hurt me, rather than to misdirect my anger toward those who have never done anything to deserve it."

Andrew could see that the man sitting opposite him was genuine in his declarations, that he truly wanted to correct his mistakes and was offering sincere contrition for his actions against Miss Bennet and his plans for his sister. Bearing in mind Elizabeth's agreement if he considered the proffered apology to be sincere, he made a decision.

"I believe that you are in earnest, Mr Lucas and, as you are, my sister will hear your apology. As I am sure you are aware, there will be a number of us in the room with her, and I do not want you to attempt to get close to her. Do you understand and accept my terms?" Andrew demanded.

"Yes, your Lordship, I absolutely accept your terms," Franklin said, while looking Andrew in the eye.

"Please wait for me here," Andrew instructed as he stood and exited the study.

"Well?" Elizabeth asked as her big brother entered the parlour.

"In my humble opinion, Sprite," he smiled at his sister, "he is sincere. However, it is still your decision, so if you do not want him to address you directly, I will tell him to put his apology in writing, which I will read before you do."

"No, Andrew, I do not want to change my mind. I believe it will be good for me to hear from Mr Lucas in person, besides all of you," she looked to her family, "will remain here with me to draw strength from, if needed."

"If that is your decision, we will have him summoned." Andrew nodded once at the door. Biggs, who had been standing station in the hall, was asked to bring the young man in the office to the parlour in five minutes.

Elizabeth was seated on a settee with her mother on one side and Andrew on the other. Father Bennet was next to his wife standing behind Elizabeth. The rest of the family sat on either side of her in a wall of protection. At the appointed time, Biggs showed Franklin into the parlour.

"Lady Elizabeth, I thank you for your condescension in agreeing to hear my apology today." He said without hesitation and Elizabeth gave a slight nod of her head. "There is no reason nor excuse for my intended behaviour towards you. It was abhorrent, and I swear that I will never behave in such a fashion again, your Ladyship." Franklin made the right decision in not trying to offer justifications for his unjustifiable behaviour. "If I may, I believe I owe your cousin, Miss Bennet, an apology as well.

"Jane is not my cousin, she is my sister," Elizabeth stated in a clear voice.

"Miss Bennet, I lied to you at your coming out ball. I did resent your choice, though, for all of the wrong reasons. I was trying to fix my own problems in the wrong way, I should never have tried to use either you or Lady Elizabeth to do so." Franklin held his breath as he waited for the responses.

"For myself, it is easy to forgive you, Mr Lucas," Jane told him. "However, if you had hurt my sister Elizabeth after all that she has endured, I would have *never* been able to grant you forgiveness. I hope that you are able to move forward and be satisfied with your life, and one day find a lady you truly love and who loves you in return." Franklin inclined his head in thanks.

"I find that your contrition is real and accept your apology. I am not ready to be in conversation with you socially, so I request that unless and until you are informed by my brother or Father Bennet, when we are at the same event that you do not approach me," Elizabeth stated.

"If it will be easier for you, as I told the Earl, I will absent myself from any event that we would attend in common," Franklin informed her.

"That will not be necessary so long as you honour my wishes," she replied with a little bit of warmth in her voice. Franklin bowed to the occupants of the parlour, wished them a good day, and made his exit.

"Someone had better inform Richard, I am sure he is plotting Mr Lucas's demise even as we speak," Will said with a grin.

"I will write to Itch," Elizabeth volunteered. "He should hear from me that I am well and have accepted the man's apology."

~~~~~~~/~~~~~~~

The next day, when Richard returned to his quarters, there was a letter waiting for him in Lizzy's hand. He opened it and read it, then reread it to make sure that he had understood the contents. Andrew and Will had both added pages to assure him that all was well, and that Lucas had been sincere. He knew that Lizzy, Andrew, and Will were all good judges of character, so he moved Franklin Lucas from the "may need to be killed' list to the 'needs to be watched' list.

Richard would do anything for his sister's protection. Elizabeth was too important to their family for him to ever allow any to harm her. He knew that George Wickham and his insane Aunt Catherine were still out there somewhere though, and he was in no way deluded that they had disappeared or left England. He was sure that at some point there would be a confrontation between the family and one or both of them.

~~~~~~~/~~~~~~~

Ian Ashby arrived at Longbourn before midday on the day he was expected. He was very impressed by what he had seen of the estate so far, as it looked like it exceeded his father's estate of Ashbury. It was certainly bigger than his brother Stephen's estate of Amberleigh. Ian knew that Lady Elizabeth and his sister

Amy were close, though unfortunately, she had not been able to join her brother on his trip to Longbourn as she was visiting a common friend of Lady Elizabeth's, Lady Loretta De Melville.

He was shown up to his chambers, two floors above the family floor and next door to the Duke of Bedford's chambers. After washing, he joined the residents in the largest drawing room prior to lunch. It did not take long for him to find Anne and for them to find seats away from the others so that they could talk while her companion, Mrs Jenkinson, kept an eye on her charge.

"Anne, I missed you so much," Ian told her softly.

"As I did you, Ian," Anne responded with pleasure.

"Please tell me that you do not require a long courtship, it has been a good number of years since I have known that I love you," he revealed.

"It is the same for me, Ian. I thought that the fates were conspiring against us each time something happened to defer my entering society. I just knew that we would not be kept apart for too long," Anne replied as she caused herself to blush at her forwardness.

"May I have a private audience with you on the morrow please, Anne?" he asked hopefully.

"Yes, Ian, you most certainly may, so long as you request permission to do so from Andrew prior." She reminded him, ensuring there would not be the minutes' delay needed after they talked.

"Then I will speak to him after the meal." As if Ashby conjured the time, the butler announced that luncheon was ready. Ashby and Anne sat next to one another and spoke between bites during the meal. At the end of the meal, Ashby was about to ask his friend for an audience when the butler announced that a courier had arrived and wished to see the Duke of Bedford.

Perry had a knowing look on his face as he went to meet the courier. He returned a few minutes later and there was a bulge in his jacket pocket. "Bennet, may I have a few minutes with my betrothed?" Perry requested.

"No more than ten minutes in my study, and the door remains half-open," Bennet allowed.

"You have already proposed, Perry, so what is this interview about?" Jane was curious.

"When I proposed, I did not have this as it was at Longfield, and then I had to wait while it was made smaller for you, my love," Perry was holding a velvet-covered box in his hand. He opened it to reveal a stunning ring. It had a large sapphire in the centre was surrounded by diamonds, none of them small, all set in what looked to Jane as if it were silver. "It is not silver, my Jane, it is platinum, which like you is very rare and precious." Perry slipped the ring onto the fourth finger of her left hand and it fit her perfectly.

"You did not have to spend so much money on me," Jane said, while admiring her ring.

"I did not buy it for you, Jane, although I would buy you anything you desire. This ring was my paternal grandmother's engagement ring. Mother used the one from her mother so this one had just been gathering dust until you came into my life and I knew that you were the one for me," he corrected her.

"But it fits perfectly, how did you know my size?" she puzzled.

"I had help from your mother, she measured one of your rings and supplied the size to me so I could have it ready for you. Unfortunately, it took longer than I would have liked to arrive in Town and then it still needed to have the size adjusted. It seems Grandmother Pearl had much larger fingers than yours." Perry drew his betrothed to himself and they used their remaining time wisely with their lips locked in a battle of which neither kept score.

On their return to the drawing room there were many exclamations over Jane's ring. Even though she was tempted, Elizabeth refrained from mentioning her sister's swollen lips and the matching set on her brother-in-law.

Ian managed to get Andrew on his own and requested that they be allowed to talk in private. After a request to Uncle Thomas, Andrew led Ashby to the study. "Let me save you some time," Andrew cut Ashby off before he could make his request.

"You want to ask my sister Anne for her hand?" Ashby nodded. "I have no objection to you marrying Anne, but there is one issue. It has only been a few weeks of courtship. If you had requested a betrothal right away, this conversation would be moot."

"I was not sure about Anne's opinion on the subject," Ashby explained.

"Now you are?" Andrew asked.

"Yes, completely," Ian confirmed.

"It is too close to the date that I granted a courtship," Seeing Ashby was about to argue, Andrew lifted his hand. "That being said, I require you to wait until after Jane and Perry's wedding. In that case, you have my permission to approach her on the day after the wedding."

"It is less than six weeks; I believe we will survive," Ashby responded.

"You had *better*!" Andrew warned. "I assume you will not want a long betrothal?" Ashby nodded his head. "I will grant a minimum of three weeks."

Ian thanked his friend and returned to share the information with Anne. She would have preferred not to wait, but she agreed that the time that Andrew demanded was not without consideration, even generous considering it had only been a few weeks of courtship they had so far enjoyed only a couple days of it in common.

CHAPTER 10

January 15, 1797

Jane could hardly contain her excitement; not just because it was her birthday, but on the morrow, she would marry Perry, and they would not have to be parted again. Yes, she would also be a Duchess, and she was happy about that, but her change in rank was nothing to the fact that she was about to marry the man that she loved. The only thing that came close in joy was that her sister had been reunited with her and her family, and in the month since Lizzy had started to call them sister and brother, she had become very close to her birth family, Jane especially. The two sisters were now so dear to one another that Lizzy would be standing up with Jane on the morrow opposite her brother who, as Perry's best friend, would be standing up with him.

The last month had flown by. They had the banns read even though acquiring a special licence would have been nothing for her betrothed. Lady Rose, who she now called Mother Rose, had assured her that she would be by Jane's side to guide her as she took up her duties as Duchess of Bedford. She had made Jane blush when she had intimated during one of their discussions that she would not object to many grandchildren to spoil most rotten.

Tammy Bennet knocked on her daughter's door and entered when she heard her daughter bid her to do so. "Jane, I cannot believe that you will be a married woman and a duchess in the morning. I will miss you so very much, but I know that Perry will always protect you and make sure that you are happy," Tammy told her oldest daughter. "How did you enjoy your birthday yesterday?"

"It was the best one that I can remember because we are a complete family again. Even though Lizzy will continue to live with her Fitzwilliam family, and we will not be in the same house, we will never be parted again. I love that she has added Bennet to her name. Elizabeth Rose Bennet Fitzwilliam; how well it sounds. Until Papa told her, she had no idea that her second name was Rose. Mother Rose was very pleased when she found out." Jane smiled as she remembered.

"Your father was overjoyed with her middle names. He told me his aim is to try and beat her in chess again—something he has not been able to do for almost a year!" Tammy smiled as she thought about how much pleasure her beloved husband had derived from Elizabeth's announcement.

"Are you here to help me calm myself before the wedding night, Mama?" Jane asked pointedly. "If you are, I must tell you I am not nervous. Although I do not know all yet, I am very much looking forward to being Perry's wife in all ways. If that makes me a wanton, so be it" Jane added defiantly.

"Oh, Janey, it does not make you a wanton, just a woman violently in love. You know the mechanics, having lived on a farm your whole life, do you not?" Tammy asked causing her daughter to blush scarlet as nodded. "Never be ashamed of what is done between the two of you in privacy—and that need not be restricted only to the night.

"It is possible that he will take pleasure in seeing all of you as you will in seeing him. That too is perfectly natural between a married couple, and nothing of which to be ashamed. The first time will hurt, possibly quite a lot, and there may be some blood as he takes your maidenhood, but after that, it will not hurt again. In fact, it will get better the more times that you repeat the act together.

"Lastly, always talk to one another about what each of you likes and dislikes. He loves you too much to ever impose something on you that you articulate as not pleasurable to you," Tammy concluded her talk with a hug of her daughter.

"Thank you, Mama, I was not nervous, but now I am looking forward to our wedding night with anticipation of pleasure both given and taken," Jane informed her mother with a tinge of pink in her cheeks.

"Try to get some sleep, Jane, or do you want to speak to Aunt Maddie before you try?" Tammy asked.

"No, Mama, I will try to sleep," Jane kissed her mother on each cheek and bade her good night.

~~~~~~~~/~~~~~~~

The Lucas parents were very grateful that their son had come to his senses and that he had not destroyed their friendship with the Bennets or ruined their name in Meryton. After his apology, Franklin had backed up his words with actions. He had thrown himself into his duties at Lucas Lodge and had not gone near the bar at the Royal Crown.

There had been two or three times that he had been in the same room with Lady Elizabeth, and other than a polite greeting to the family, he had kept away. The last time, her brother Richard Fitzwilliam had been present. Luckily for Franklin, Richard had not found his behaviour lacking, so there was no reason to 'talk' to him again.

There had been a dinner hosted at Lucas Lodge that had been attended by the Bennets and their guests. Sir William had been beside himself hosting a Duke; an Earl and Countess; and a Dowager Duchess and Countess. Franklin had been in the receiving line and greeted Lady Elizabeth like he did everyone else. Even in his own home, he kept to his word.

Due to his now exemplary behaviour, his name was not removed from the wedding invitation. He would be at the church and subsequent wedding breakfast with his family, and he was bound and determined that he would continue to behave in a way that was above reproach.

~~~~~~~/~~~~~~~

Elizabeth was in the sitting room between her chambers and Georgiana's, which was a few down from where Jane and her mother were having their discussion. Aggie was curled up in front of the fire, snoring away. Being at Longbourn with both her families around her was the happiest that she had felt since her beloved father was murdered. Any time that she would start to allow her self-created guilt to intrude, which was very seldom these days, she would hear her Papa's words and the promise he extracted from her, followed by her family's words of love. She knew that one day, many years in the future, she would see her Papa once again in heaven. She ruminated about the conversation that she had with her Fitzwilliam and Darcy family about ten days earlier.

The family, excluding Alex, had met in Andrew and Marie's sitting room. Richard was with them for the weekend.

"Lizzy, you asked us to meet you here?" her mother asked.

"Yes, I did. I have been thinking about something, my name!" Elizabeth saw the looks of consternation and quickly move to reassure her family. "I am not *desirous of removing a name, it is adding two that I am talking about."*

Everyone, her mother especially, had relaxed at her assurance that she had not changed her mind about being a Fitzwilliam. "What is it that you are thinking of Lizzy?" Aunt Anne asked.

"Do you remember that Father Bennet told me that my middle name is Rose as he named me Elizabeth Rose for Grandmother Elizabeth Rose Bennet?" There were nods all around. "I was thinking of adding Rose and Bennet between Elizabeth and Fitzwilliam. Bennet will be like a middle name, regardless of where I was birthed, I am and always will be a Fitzwilliam, well unless I marry one day, and even then, it will not change who my family is."

"That sounds like a good name for you, Sprite," Richard offered.

"Thank you, Itch, I think so too," Elizabeth answered.

"I hate to say it," Will said with a grin, "as much as I hate to agree with my much *older cousin, it sounds fine."*

There was no dissention within the family. Elaine hugged her daughter tightly. The family group joined the Bennets and young Alex in the drawing room where Elizabeth announced her new name to all. Just like he had when she had called him 'Father Bennet' the first time, Bennet had moisture in his eyes.

Elizabeth was snapped out of her reverie when Georgiana stuck her head into their shared sitting room to confirm that it was only Lizzy present. "Come in, Gigi, it is only Aggie with me in here." Aggie lifted her head on mention of her name and once she saw who was visiting her mistress, she put her head down and went back to pleasant snore-producing dreams.

"Can you believe that Jane will be a Duchess on the morrow," Georgiana asked excitedly.

"It does seem unreal, but I can tell you from talking to Jane that she would have married Perry title or not. She is marrying for the only good reason to marry, the deepest love," Elizabeth informed her younger cousin.

"I believe that Andrew's restriction on Mr Ashby to propose to Anne is over the day after the wedding. Just do not go off and marry someone who will take you to the other side of the country Lizzy, I do not know what I would do without you," Georgiana begged.

"I will keep that in mind after I come out, Gigi," Elizabeth smiled. If her wishes were granted and her feelings were returned, then she might live close—very close—to her cousin, and they mayhap would be sisters.

For her part, Lady Elaine felt much relief after the meeting when Lizzy had announced her name change, the last vestiges of doubt that her daughter would change her mind about where she was to live slipped away. She had breathed a sigh of relief as she understood what Lizzy wanted to do—she was stating for all to hear that part of her was a Bennet, but she was and always would be a Fitzwilliam.

Thomas Bennet was beyond happy at his second daughter's decision. It was far more than he had ever expected.

~~~~~~~/~~~~~~~

Anne had been counting the days ever since Ian had informed her that he had Andrew's permission to ask for her hand—they only had to wait until after Jane's and Perry's wedding. She had started crossing days off the calendar with the seventeenth day of January circled so much the number was all but illegible.
~~~~~~~

Until she met and then fell in love with Ian, she did not know that it was possible to love another the way that she loved him. While ruminating on what was soon to come, she thought back to the woman who had given birth to her. She had tried to claim that Anne was too sickly and that she would not be able to marry, except to someone she chose who would *understand*. Anne was now aware that she was as healthy as anyone else and that the woman had sprouted that nonsense so that if she chose to one day kill Anne, she would have a plausible reason for her death.

With his will, her father had gifted her with the best family that a girl could want and had secured Rosings for her, making it impossible for his wife to touch any estate funds. She did not remember her first father as he had died when she was but a few years old, but her second father she had loved, known, and remembered. She was sad that when she did marry Father Reggie would not be there to walk her down the aisle, but Andrew would stand in his stead. With Andrew, Richard, and Lizzy, she had the best of siblings and was never alone.

Mrs Jenkinson, who had saved her from her mother, was still with her. She had gone from nursemaid, to governess, and then finally to companion, and Anne loved her like a second mother after Mother Elaine. It was already decided that when she and Ian married, they would reside at Rosings and Mrs Jenkinson would be given a sizable cottage on a few acres of land, and would also be provided with a very generous pension to live out the remainder of her life in comfort.

Anne loved Elaine as well as any daughter could love her mama and had only kept the de Bourgh name to honour her first father. She would have been Lady Anne Fitzwilliam had she not wanted to keep her first father's name alive. As she teased with her dry wit at the time, it would have been too confusing with two Lady Anne's in the family. While she was exceedingly happy for Jane, she could not wait for her wedding to be over, so that they could get to the day that Ian would propose.

~~~~~~~/~~~~~~~
~~~~~~~

The morning of the wedding of Jane Bennet and Perry Rhys-Davies was a clear and frigid winter day. There was a layer of snow on the ground. When Perry awoke to gentle shaking by his valet at Bennington Fields where he was residing with the De Melvilles, Ashby, and some other families, he almost jumped out of bed. It was the day that he was to marry the woman that he loved.

A little after nine, he was pacing back and forth in the drawing room when the Fitzwilliam brothers, Charles Bingley, Will, William Bennet, and John Manning arrived. "I expected you earlier," Perry barked as anxiety took hold of him.

"We do not have to leave for at least ten minutes brother," Andrew told him as he put his hand on his arm to stop the frenetic pacing back and forth. "We have to be at Longbourn's church by half after nine, as it is we will be there before that time, so calm yourself, or do I have to ask my assistants here to hold you down?" he threatened his friend in jest.

That seemed to reach Perry, and he calmed down, concentrating on how his Jane would look as she walked toward him that day. The ten minutes seemed to drag by, but they finally entered the coaches that would take him to the church and his heart.

~~~~~~~/~~~~~~~

Jane was ready by half after the hour, even with her mother and Aunts Maddie and Hattie fussing over her. She was wearing a white silk dress with empire waist and puffed-up sleeves. It was very tasteful and modest, even for the fashions of the day. There was a transparent organza overlay that flowed into a longer back piece, which formed a train. The overlay and her delicate veil were lightly decorated with oblong pearls. She wore a strand of pearls around her neck with teardrop pearl and diamond earbobs. When she descended the grand stairs, she truly looked like an angel from on high.

Mrs Hill was quietly crying as she watched one of her girls preparing to marry. Even more wonderful was that Miss Lizzy was with her older sister, the two of them together on this day was a source for much joy. Elizabeth was waiting in the entrance
~~~~~~~

hall for her sister, gazing at her with the same wonder the rest of the ladies and her father gaped at her with.

Tammy, James, Kitty, and Tom all kissed Jane, then they and the aunts left the house to make the short walk to the church, just to one side of the manor house. After Elizabeth checked all was well with the dress and the veil was in place, she helped Jane don a warm coat for the short walk, then with her father on one side and her younger sister on the other, Jane Bennet left the house that she had lived in these last eighteen years for the final time as a Bennet.

When Martha Bingley and the Hursts arrived at the church, they were welcomed by their friends and others who lived in the area. After helping escort Perry to the church Charles joined the family in their pew.

Perry was standing in his place at the front of the church when he saw his very soon to be mother-in-law and her three younger children take their seats next to William and John in the front pew. After a brief pause, the door to the vestibule opened and a radiant Elizabeth made her way slowly up the aisle.

As Will watched her from his seat next to his parents and siblings, his heart prayed that one day it would be him standing at the front of the church while she walked toward him. He suspected that Wes De Melville may have similar wishes, and he did not have any idea where Lizzy's preferences laid, or even if she had any.

Mr Pierce indicated that the congregation, with more Peers than had ever been seen by the citizens of the area, stand. The door to the vestibule opened again and Jane entered on her father's arm. Perry had not seen anything more beautiful in his life than the vision of his bride to be as she walked toward him.

He advanced a few steps and met Bennet, who lifted the veil to kiss his daughter's cheek and then placed her hand on Perry's arm. Once they were standing in front of the rector, he signalled the congregation to be seated. The service flew by and neither bride nor groom remembered reciting their vows. Before they knew it, Mr Pierce pronounced them man and wife, and they were led to the rectory to sign the parish's register. Once they had signed, Andrew and Elizabeth left them alone.

"My wife," Perry murmured as he kissed his wife.

"My husband," Jane replied breathlessly as she yearned for more kisses.

Knowing that the family was waiting for them in the church, they shared but one more, then returned toward the waiting arms of the well-wishers. As they emerged from the rectory, they were mobbed by their family with everyone trying to 'your Grace' Jane first. Elizabeth hugged her sister tightly."

"Jane, we are now sisters and sisters-in-law," she teased.

"Silly, I am still only your sister," Jane returned. "By your logic, or lack thereof, Perry is now your brother-in-law twice over."

"Technically, he is!" came the pert reply.

"Please, family and friends who have known me all of my life, Jane will suffice, not my title. You call Perry by his name, so I demand the same!" Jane scolded her family playfully.

"We have got used to having a Duke around, even a Dowager Duchess, but we have yet to accustom ourselves to being in the exalted company of a Duchess," James drawled with an exaggerated bow that earned him a playful slap on the arm from his sister. Marie then hugged her new sister tightly. She had been an only daughter, but now she had, between her marriage and Perry's, gained a slew of siblings.

The Bingleys and the Hursts had waited at the back of the church until the newlyweds had a free moment. They wished the Duke and his new Duchess happy and then boarded the carriage that would return them to Netherfield. Martha was sad that Oscar had not been there to see such a wonderful wedding. Her grieving was still very raw, and she knew it would take her a while before she started to feel the full measure of emotions such as happiness and enjoyment.

Once the well wishes of the immediate family were completed, all except Jane and Perry walked back to Longbourn. The couple would wait five minutes and then follow to allow everyone to settle in the ballroom before they were announced as a married couple for the first time. They stood staring at one another and only by the happenstance of a servant coming in to clean around the alter did they recall themselves and leave at the appointed time.

"Will you not tell me where we are to go for our wedding trip, husband?" Jane asked, not for the first time.

"You will find out on the morrow, my wife, whom I love above all others," Perry answered.

"So it begins with secrets," Jane teased him sweetly.

"I give you my oath, Duchess, that the *only* secrets I will ever keep from you are when they are a surprise for you," Perry assured his wife in earnest.

They made the quick walk to the house and handed their outerwear to the footman waiting for them as they entered. When they arrived at the doors to the ballroom, two footmen swung the doors open and Mr Hill had the distinct pleasure of announcing: "Their Graces, the Duke and Duchess of Bedford." The response was a round of thunderous applause.

One of the first to wish them happiness was the Lucas family, including Franklin, who sincerely wished them joy and refrained from using Jane's familiar name as he had been wont to do in the past. The greeting between the couple and the family were as warm as could be and the message to all was clear, whatever had happened in the past was water under the bridge, and there was no animosity between anyone present and Franklin Lucas.

Elizabeth, her brothers, and sister Anne added an exclamation mark to the complete redemption of the Lucas heir when he was greeted cordially by all, during which Lady Elizabeth had spoken a few words to him with a smile on her face.

Two and a half hours later, Jane was changed into her travelling clothes and joined her husband in the drawing room to wish their families farewell. They had hardly eaten anything, but they had no need to worry, Mrs Hill had placed a hamper full of comestibles in the carriage along with flagons of various drinks.

Mother Rose hugged her new daughter tightly, telling her that she was the perfect wife for her son. The night before the wedding, she had again pledged any support and help that Jane may find that she needed as she learnt her duties of mistress and duchess. She and Perry were hugged by all in the extended family, one of the last to hug their Jane was Elizabeth.

"I will miss you so much 'aney," Elizabeth hugged her sister tightly.

"You will be missed too, Lizzy, but now that we are reunited we shall never lose one another again," Jane promised.

"I have a feeling that you will not be thinking of me or anyone else very much over the three months of your wedding trip aside with Perry," came her impertinent rejoinder.

"Lizzy!" Jane blushed scarlet, but could not deny the truth of her sister's words.

Next Tammy hugged her daughter while Bennet shook his new son's hand, and then they swapped. Perry received a warm hug from his mother-in-law who received a kiss on her cheek for her troubles, while Jane was enfolded in her dear father's arms."

"You will do very well together, Jane," he told her quietly. "I pity the servant who tries to cheat you. You know that I could have never parted with you to one less worthy. He is a very good man."

"Yes, Papa, he is, but to me, he is the best of men," Jane corrected her father.

The newlyweds mounted their carriage, and as waves were both given and received, it was jerked into motion by the team of six matched horses. The family stood and watched until the coach disappeared around the bend in the drive.

CHAPTER 11

March 1797

Now that she and the family were aware of her true birthday, she would be sixteen in two days. There was a bonus! Elizabeth and Georgiana shared a birthday, so they would have a joint celebration at Pemberley.

Elizabeth, she thought smiled as about how reluctant her birth brothers William and James had been to return to their respective schools. The two had departed to Cambridge and Eton, the day after their sister's wedding to Perry in January, which was also the day her sister Anne had become betrothed to Ian Ashby.

Anne was now a married woman for less than a month. As it was still cold in the north, she and her new husband Ian had gratefully accepted Uncle George and Aunt Anne's offer to honeymoon at Seaview Cottage. They would make time to visit Lake View House when it was warmer. Elizabeth and Georgie had both stood up for Anne, while Ian's brother had done the honours for him, having returned in time for the wedding, from his own wedding trip.

Thoughts of wedding trips made her think of Jane. In one of the few letters that had arrived, Jane had gushed about how they were on Perry's private ship and were making a tour of the Mediterranean Coast, except France, where the great terror still gripped that country. In the same letter, the new Duchess had told her sister and asked her to pass on to her brothers, sisters, and cousins, that all gifts she purchased for her family on her wedding trip would be presented to them when she and Perry returned from their wedding trip.

Jane had also written that she hoped they might return before the family all met up with the newlywed Ashbys at Rosings in April for Easter.

There was a positive result when Anne and Ian departed on their trip. The Earl of Ashbury allowed his daughter Amy, who was fifteen, to accept an invitation to stay with her new sister-in-law until the families all met in Kent for Easter.

Andrew and Marie were blissfully happy. The only thing that marred Marie's happiness somewhat was that she was not increasing yet. Her mother, who was with them at Snowhaven keeping Elaine company, had urged her not to be concerned, telling her daughter that she had been wed four years before she was with child with Perry, and Mother Elaine had shared that it had been more than three years for her. It was four months to their fourth anniversary and Marie prayed that it would not be too much longer before she began to increase.

Elizabeth missed her cousin Will and was expecting his arrival in time for the joint birthday at his home. They had written and discussed books via the post, but it was just not the same as being in each other's company. Elizabeth had no wish to deny that she was hopelessly in love with her cousin, but she was unsure of his feelings and understood that she should not try to ascertain his feelings until she was out—which was still two long years from now.

Elizabeth was aware that Wes De Melville, Viscount Westmore, seemed to have tender feelings for her based on the attention he paid her. He always stayed within the bounds of propriety, but she was not blind. What she did not know was that she was only blind when it came to knowing how her cousin Will felt about her. She liked Wes, but as a friend and nothing more. If she had shared her feelings with Mrs Annesley, she might have had it pointed out to her, just how unobservant she was to her cousin's feelings for her.

The Bennets were enjoying their time at Snowhaven immensely. Bennet did spend time in the large library, but the most pleasure that he derived was furthering his knowledge of his daughter's life over the last fifteen years. The more he learned, the more certain he was that she had been discovered and adopted by the perfect family. Even though he had never met Lizzy's Papa in person, he could feel the late Earl's presence in the home.

Each day that they spent together brought the family closer. As Bennet was sitting in the library, he could not but remember the first visit of a sennight's length that the Snowhaven party had spent at Pemberley in early February.

George Darcy had purposely not mentioned the library for the first few hours after the Bennets and Fitzwilliams had changed and joined the family in the drawing room. It was not too long before Georgiana and Alex led their cousins outdoors, once they bundled up, to go look at the horses in the Darcy stables with Biggs, Johns, and Mrs Annesley not far behind.

Right on cue, Lady Anne Darcy invited Tammy and Bennet to join her and her housekeeper, Mrs Reynolds, for a tour of the house. George could not miss Bennet's look of disappointment of there being no mention of the library. Bennet did not know it, but that was where the tour would terminate. George Darcy was waiting for the Bennets in front of double doors as his wife excused her housekeeper.

"I thought I would join you for the last part of the tour," George built his friend's suspense. He decided it was enough and he and his wife each pulled a door open and watched him, certain few would ever get the chance to see such an unguarded reaction from Mr Thomas Bennet.

As Bennet stepped into the room, he thought he had died and entered Nirvana. The smell of leather filled his lungs as his eyes tried to take in the sheer number of tomes!

The library was immense! The bottom level was larger than the largest ballroom Bennet had seen, and *there were two more levels above it! There were four spiral staircases that allowed one to gain access between them, and the upper two floors had a wide companionway, so one could peruse the books. The books and items of wonder were stacked floor to ceiling on all three levels, so each section had a ladder on rollers to reach the upper shelves.*

Throughout the space were tables and comfortable leather armchairs. Bennet surmised that if had he ten lifetimes, he would not be able to read half of the books arrayed before him. "The descriptions that I had heard hardly did the reality justice, Darcy," he stated in awe.

"We do have a slight advantage over most," George admitted, "When my first ancestor, Pierre D'Arcy, was awarded Pemberley by William the Conqueror, he had a large collection in French; you see them in the glass cases," George pointed out. "The reverence for the written word started with him, and every subsequent master over many generations added to the collection, this one included, and thus we have arrived at the point that you behold before us."

"Thomas, are we going to see you while we are at Pemberley?" Tammy asked only half in jest.

"That all depends on whether the Darcys are willing to supply me with a bed in this incredible library of theirs," Bennet re-joined. He did spend time in the library alone, but not at the exclusion of activities with the family. A good few hours were spent in the library with Lizzy, and it is there they started debating books, bringing them even closer than they already were becoming.

Bennet grinned as he remembered how his friend had made him wait to see the room he wanted to see above all others. He had to think of a way to return the favour. He did not have an idea yet, but he knew one would come, given enough time.

~~~~~~~/~~~~~~~

Greg Jones had done as his secret employer had asked. He had kept his nose clean and out of trouble, save the one time in Kympton when his friend John Branch had saved his hide. During one of the Fitzwilliams and Bennets visits to the estate, Jones received a note from his 'brother' to meet him in the tavern in Kympton. Jones had forgotten that he had told Branch almost a year earlier that he had no living family, so when he told his friend that he was going to request some time off from the stable master to meet his brother, Branch's suspicions were immediately raised.

Employing the skills he had learnt in the army, Branch fol-
~~~~~~~

lowed Jones discreetly. After Jones entered the Galloping Stallion Inn in Kympton, he waited a minute and then followed his quarry. He saw Jones sit in a booth. The next one was empty, so Branch slid into it.

"Ya were not followed, were ya?" the man Jones was meeting asked. This unknown person was eventually discovered to be one of Mrs Fitzpatrick's footmen.

"Nah, no one suspe'ts nothin'," Jones returned confidently.

"Ya bin' there for a long time, she wants you to start gatherin' informat'n about the family's movements, 'specially when both Darcys and Fitzwilliams be travlin' together," his contact relayed the instructions.

"That be easy fir me ta get," Jones boasted, "I be friends wif a man 'o be an assistant to the driver o' the Darcy's coach!"

"I am to return every fortnight. There be a big chestnut tree on t'e green. On t'e one side there be a knot'ole wif a piece o' wood that 'ides it. Put notes in there fir me." The man started to get up, Branch made like he was asleep with a half-finished tankard of ale in his hand in case the man saw him. He did not, and as Jones remained to finish his ale, Branch took the opportunity to slip out of the inn, after which he saw the contact mount his horse and take off towards the south. Branch made haste back to Pemberley. He needed to see the master.

When he arrived back at the estate, he entered through the kitchens and asked Mr Douglas to request an audience with the master on his behalf. Douglas returned and ushered him via the servant corridors to the master's study. He related all to the master who told him that he had done very well and instructed him to keep as close to this Jones as possible. Once Branch departed and headed back to the stables, George had his butler find Lord Matlock and Mr Bennet to request that they join him in his study.

Once he finished telling them what the incognito guard had relayed, Andrew let out a rare invective for him. "It has to be our former aunt!" he surmised.

"I agree, Andrew," his uncle replied. "If it is her, this is exactly the underhanded type of thing that she would attempt to try to punish us for her perceived grievances."

"Former aunt?" Bennet asked.

"Yes, Anne Ashby's former mother…" George told Bennet all about the 'venerable' and clearly insane Lady Catherine de Bourgh.

"You know, Uncle George, when that murderer George Wickham disappeared, he had no funds just the shirt on his back, I would wager that those two miscreants have somehow found their way to each other!" Andrew spat out.

"What do you intend to do?" Bennet asked.

"As they have no idea, we know who their spy is, and he is being carefully watched, we will allow this to play out for some time and hopefully net both murderers at once," George informed them. "With this Jones being so confident that Branch believes him, we will funnel information we want our adversaries to know through him, then we will put a plan in place when we learn of what will be attempted."

Andrew and Bennet agreed with the plan of action. Soon after, the three men returned to the rest of the family and shared what they knew with their wives, Elaine, and the older children.

When Jones walked back into their shared sleeping quarters, Branch asked him how his meeting with his brother was. Jones apparently was comfortable lying to people because he didn't hesitate to say that he had enjoyed his meal with his brother, Phillip. Branch started his campaign to get closer to the Trojan horse in their midst, even as Jones continued to believe that getting information from Branch would be a breeze.

~~~~~~~/~~~~~~~

When her footman reported to her on his return, for once Mrs Fitzpatrick was not displeased. After all the years of waiting, the pieces were finally falling into place, and she would soon show her ex-family that they should never have disrespected her. She had not informed him yet, but Wickham would have a role to play in her plan.

'*At last,*' she told herself, '*I will get my revenge, and then I will*
~~~~~~~

take all that is due me!' Her daughter and her new husband were not excluded. *'When I have dealt with the Darcys and Fitzwilliams, the Ashbys will be next. How dare they steal my estate from me!'*

Unfortunately, her insanity had deepened over the course of her isolation. She ignored the fact that even if she did succeed in killing anyone, she would have no way to access their funds. And while the murder of the maid was a memory long forgotten for her, no one else had removed it from the list of things she would be required to answer for.

George Wickham had been incensed when he had read of his half-sister's marriage. Rosings was lost to him! The fact that he had never had a way of claiming it did not enter into the equation for him, for it was what he was owed, and that was all he needed to consider. He knew that the old lady was getting ready to unleash her revenge against the Darcys and Fitzwilliams, and hoped that she would allow him to play a role.

If he were, he further hoped that he would get to fulfil his deepest desire of finishing the job he had attempted all those years ago and kill Lady Elizabeth Fitzwilliam. Finding out that she was not a mongrel had only made him hate her more. He fantasised about watching the life fade from her eyes as he choked the life out of her. He would have to intensify his search for the old lady's fortune so that he would be able to escape England as soon as the deed was done.

~~~~~~~/~~~~~~~

With the help from his friend Darcy, in the more than two months since his father's death, Charles Bingley was starting to manage all aspects of his estate. Darcy, although tempted to do so at times, had not jumped in and done things himself, limiting himself to the giving of advice as needed and when requested. The two friends, along with Mr Nicholas Church who was Netherfield's steward, were in the study planning the spring planting before Darcy was scheduled to depart for Pemberley to attend the joint birthday celebrations of his sister and cousin. Hurst sat in on most of their meetings, and except for the occasional question remained unobtrusive, but he too was learning a
~~~~~~~

lot.

Will was impressed at how Charles no longer relied on others to make decisions for him as he fully assumed his new role as head of his small family. Both Darcy and Mr Church advised him on matters. He asked a lot of good questions, then made the final decision on his own. If either man thought that his decision was wrong, he no longer accepted it at face value and approve the change, they would have to show their reasoning to be sound, and the consequences were considered for making the change or choosing not to.

Will was grateful that it was not him that was thrust into his inheritance at such a young age. He was so thankful that his father was still very much hale and healthy, and that he had not had to experience the pain that Bingley, Andrew, and Rich had suffered. He tried to imagine how different he would have been had that come to pass, pulling himself from his maudlin thoughts he thanked God that he did not have to learn the answers to those morbid questions.

Martha was well pleased to have the three Hursts and her mother with her, so she would not be alone with her grief for the long hours that her son was busy learning from his friend. The only times the burden of grief lifted was when she was entertaining her granddaughter. Mary had the Hurst's colouring, brown eyes with dark hair. If one did not know better, they would mistake her for a sister of Lady Elizabeth Fitzwilliam or Kitty Bennet. At two and some months there were signs that she would be precocious, intelligent and a very curious young girl.

Louisa had not told anyone yet, but she was increasing again, she wanted to feel the quickening first, which she estimated would be in the next month or two. Her mother shot her knowing glances but did not say anything, waiting for her daughter to come to her.

Charlotte Pierce and her daughter Emma were almost daily visitors. Her already deep friendship with Louisa became deeper still. Emma and Mary played together like sisters and were never happy when it was time for Charlotte to enter her gig and return to the parsonage. On days that the weather was inclement, Louisa would send one of their carriages to collect and return her and Mary's friends.

Will was very much looking forward to departing for Pemberley the following morning. He missed all his family members, but there was one that he missed above all others—Elizabeth. He loved her, and being distant from her just made his heart ache so much more. The less than two years to her come out seemed like millennia to him. He was still questioning her feelings for him and was worried about what he had gleaned from his mother's letters where she had mentioned that his friend Wes had been spending a lot of time around Elizabeth. The morrow and the next day of travel could not pass fast enough so that he would be able to see her again.

~~~~~~~/~~~~~~~

"You know, Lizzy, if I am ever in need of a horse and none are available, I would be able to ride Aggie," Amy teased as they rode across a field at Pemberley with Georgiana and her younger sister Kitty with Aggie loping along in between Saturn and Brown Beauty. At eleven, Kitty felt very privileged to be allowed to accompany her older sister and cousins for such adventures.

"I think that you may be a little too big for Aggie now," Elizabeth returned.

"You are not calling me rotund, are you Lizzy!" Amy shot back while she smiled.

"I would never dare," came the impertinent reply.

"I see that your brothers arrived today," Amy observed.

"Yes, two of our Bennet side brothers. Richard arrives on the morrow," Lizzy informed her friend.

"William arrives on the morrow as well," Georgiana added.

"I know that, Gigi!" Elizabeth blushed. Her reaction was not missed by Amy or Georgiana who looked at one another knowingly.

"Look!" exclaimed Kitty. "There are Papa, James, and Tom." Kitty pointed to the three riders crossing the meadow ahead of them. The four young ladies wheeled their horses and increased
~~~~~~~

speed to catch up to the three Bennet men.

~~~~~~~~/~~~~~~~~

Branch had let it drop near Jones one evening, as they were preparing to sleep that he needed to be able to send more money to his ailing mother, so he would have to find ways to earn more funds.

Jones had responded by informing his 'friend' that he may know of a job that would pay him over one hundred pounds. Branch had pretended to salivate over such a sum and Jones told him to be patient, that he would call on him soon.

~~~~~~~~/~~~~~~~~

As planned, Richard and Will had met at an inn on the Great North Road and travelled the rest of the distance to Pemberley together from there. It was perfect for Richard, as he only had to ride his horse a short distance until he was in the warm, well sprung, and comfortable Darcy carriage. It was above five in the afternoon on their second day of travel when they entered the courtyard at Pemberley. Will surveyed the welcoming committee and was disappointed that Elizabeth was not among those welcoming him home.

Just then from out of the house's doors there was a streak of yellow with raven coloured hair trailing behind it, followed by a light blue one with blonde hair as Elizabeth launched herself into her brother's open arms with Georgiana doing the same to Will.

"It has been far too long, Richard!" Elizabeth chastised him in jest, "We have seen hide nor hair of you since Jane's and Perry's wedding!"

"It is the Army, Lizzy; I cannot abscond anytime that the fancy takes me. They take a very dim view of absenting one's self without leave or, as it would be after three days, desertion!" Richard told her as he admired his sister. She was certainly not his little sister any longer, and if the way that William was staring at her was any indication, his youthful infatuation with her mind had grown into full-blown romantic love.

"Who is this tall young lady I see before me?" William teased his sister.

"Oh, do be serious, Will," Georgiana scolded. "You know it is me."

The two were welcomed by the rest of the family and were soon on their way up to their chambers to wash and change for dinner. If Will thought Elizabeth was irresistible before, he realised that even after less than three months; she was even more beautiful and womanly looking than she was when he last saw her. He would need to seek his parent's advice again.

CHAPTER 12

Elizabeth would always remember her sixteenth birthday as the happiest one to date. Alongside, the Fitzwilliams and Darcys were Lady Rose and her birth family. The only ones missing were Perry and Jane, and Anne and Ian, both couples still enjoying their wedding trips. It was also the first year in her memory that her birthday was being celebrated on the day that she was actually born.

To add to her joy, she and her closest cousin shared a birthday. Georgiana was thirteen and looking more like a young lady than a girl with each day that passed. In July, Georgiana would be going to a school for young ladies in London. Lizzy had never been sent to school because in her family's opinion, thanks to her intelligence and non-traditional education, that kind of school would have been a waste of time for her.

The chocolate cake had three-tiered layers. The bottom tier had seventeen candles for Elizabeth, while between the middle and the top, there were fourteen candles for Georgiana. They started blowing out candles opposite one another and both moved clockwise around the cake until all one and thirty candles were extinguished.

Bennet had moisture in his eyes while Tammy squeezed his arm. The last birthday he had attended for his Lizzy was fifteen years ago. All the progress they had made at melding their two families was heart-warming and, considering that he never expected to see his second daughter again in this lifetime, was beyond anything that he could have imagined.

One daughter was a duchess and the other was raised the daughter of an earl. He could not imagine it if he had tried. Who would Kitty marry; a prince? The thought of his youngest marrying made him maudlin. William and John knew what he wanted and with the sale of Netherfield plus the five thousand he had added, they each had a legacy of fifty thousand pounds generating income invested with Gardiner and Associates.

Bennet was sorry that neither the Gardiners nor the Phillips were able to join them at Pemberley or Snowhaven, but both families would be present at Rosings Park. His sister Maddie was increasing with her second child, and Easter would be the last time Maddie would be able to travel any distance until after she recovered from her upcoming confinement.

William watched Elizabeth with supreme pleasure as she tucked into her oversized slice of cake. He had the conversation with his parents the previous night.

Will had knocked on his parents' sitting-room door, and when summoned inside he had joined them in a glass of wine in front of the crackling fire. "I need your advice," he opened. After his blunder years ago, he had sworn to be open with his parents and ask their advice if in a quandary.

"Is it about a certain extremely intelligent cousin by any chance?" his mother asked with an indulgent smile.

"How did you know? Am I that transparent?" Will was embarrassed that his parents had noticed his problem.

"Yes, you are. Do you realise just how often you stare at Lizzy when you are together?" George asked. "The way you stare at her so intently while trying to not appear as if you are, be careful that Lizzy does not think that you are seeking fault in her!"

"It is the opposite; I find her perfection personified! I love her, not like I loved her mind then, but as a woman; as the woman, the only woman that I would ever want to bind my life to!" Will laid his feelings bare for his parents.

"You are aware that Andrew will not even consider an application to court her, never mind a request for her hand until after she has at least experienced some of her first season," his mother informed him.

"I am well aware of that, but I do not know how she feels about me! I know that Wes De Melville is interested in her, mayhap he is

better for her," he returned weakly.

"If you truly believe that, then you do not deserve her love, William," George admonished his son.

"It is hard not knowing," William whined unbecomingly.

"If the way she looks at you is any indication, then I have a feeling that Lizzy will be my daughter one day," Lady Anne soothed her son, who gaped at her in disbelieving surprise.

He was snapped out of his reverie thinking of the young woman that he loved by someone handing him a plate of cake, he decided that he would have to be a lot more observant of his cousin Elizabeth.

After the presents were opened, Will and Richard met with George Darcy, Andrew, and Bennet in the master's study. They were informed of what Branch had learned from the stable hand Jones, how Jones now thought that Branch was working with him to achieve his employer's aim, and how they believed that said employer was none other than Lady Catherine.

Richard, of course, wanted to head for the stables and force the location of his former Aunt from the man, but he was able to see the wisdom of the plan that had been formulated. Both Andrew and Uncle George promised Richard and Will faithfully that they would be apprised of any new developments.

~~~~~~~/~~~~~~~

Branch followed Jones into Kympton on the night before his accomplice was to return to pick up his note. The note Jones carried read: *Nothing to report.* The master wanted to keep the ones that requested the intelligence interested, and Branch was sure that Jones' employer had never seen his writing before, or if he or she had, they had not paid attention to it.

After Jones removed the loose knot of wood and deposited his note, he left. Branch gave him fifteen minutes before opening the hiding place and switched the notes. As he left, he nodded to one of his fellow guards who the master had installed in quarters which had a clear view of the tree, and more especially the knothole.

The next day as the sun rose, the watcher observed a man
~~~~~~~

look around to make sure he was unobserved. He opened the cover, removed the note, and closed the hole again. The man slipped away, and a few minutes later a horse left the inn heading south. The man wrote a report and handed it to a boy, one of the tenant's sons, to ride back to the estate and deliver the note to the master.

The master had decided against trying to follow the man on horseback to his source, as even a dim man would eventually notice he was being followed over many miles of road. Until instructed otherwise, the guard would be at his post every fortnight to observe, unless Branch discovered a change in the schedule.

~~~~~~~/~~~~~~~

Mrs Fitzpatrick was in anticipation of her footman returning from Derbyshire. When he finally arrived, she held out her hand for the piece of rolled-up parchment. She read it and then threw it into the fire. It read:

4 April – both families Rosings Park, Kent. Many outriders.

There would be no chance to put her plan into motion, not with the outriders and on the Great North Road that was so well travelled. No, as much as she hated to, she would have to wait a little longer, but at least she had her spy in place and no one was any wiser.

George Wickham too was frustrated; he had discovered where the old bat kept her fortune…in the bank! How was he to access her money from the bank? Thanks to her suspicious nature, he was sure that she had instructed the bank that she and she alone was to be there in person to withdraw money. Now his puzzle became how to make her want to withdraw a large sum.

He was at a loss on what to do, but he was confident in his ability to charm, so he started to strategize. He had lost what he considered his birthright, Rosings Park, so it was imperative that he succeed in getting his hands on her fortune.

~~~~~~~/~~~~~~~

April 1797

Elizabeth was looking forward to hugging Anne and her new brother Ian. She was in the second carriage that turned into Rosings from the lane just after they passed the Hunsford Parsonage. Mr David Bamber, his wife, and their three sons were all enjoying the spring weather in their garden and had waved to the carriages as they passed their house.

It was frustrating that the view of those waiting was obscured by the first coach. Elizabeth, Amy, Georgiana, William, and John alighted from the carriage. As soon as Elizabeth heard Aunt Rose proclaim "Perry" she knew that Jane too had come. She picked up her skirts and ran toward the entrance, where she spied Jane in a hug with Mother Bennet. She waited patiently until Jane had hugged her father, then she fell into her sister's arms.

"How well you look, Jane," Elizabeth gushed as she held onto her sister as if she had been gone for years, not months.

"I missed you too, Lizzy," Jane smiled at her sister.

"It is good of you to say so, but I have a feeling that your husband kept you busy so you did not have too much time to think of us," Lizzy stated innocently.

"Lizzy!" Jane blushed deep scarlet.

"What did I say?" Lizzy asked as she saw anyone who was or had been married trying to hold back their laughs. "I meant that you had so much to see, so I am not sure..." Her mouth made a perfect 'O' as she realised how what she had said could also have been heard. As soon as it hit her, Elizabeth joined Jane in blushing, and those who had tried to hold back their laughing failed.

Anne introduced her housekeeper and butler, the same couple that her mother and Aunt Anne had hired, Mr and Mrs Firth, and asked them to make sure that all the guests and their trunks arrived at the correct chambers. Before going up to her chambers, Amy was pleased to see her parents and her older brother and wife. After greeting the rest of her family, she was shown to her chambers in the suite that she shared with Lizzy. Georgiana and Kitty were in the next suite across from William and John, who were placed next to James and Tom.

As her lady's maid Thénardier was changing her, Elizabeth was sad that Will would not be joining them as he would be spending Easter with the Bingleys and their friends in the Meryton area. At least she had seen the object of her love at Pemberley for Gigi's and her birthdays.

The following day, the De Melvilles joined the party at Rosings. From Elizabeth's perspective, it was a mixed blessing. Retta, who was fifteen, would be joining them, but so would Wes. She did not know how to deflect his attention, and she could say nothing to him as it would be a highly inappropriate conversation for a girl not out to have with a man.

The following morning Elizabeth decided to take one of her long rambles before the sun rose, accompanied by Aggie and Johns. Before she exited the house, she went to the kitchens and was rewarded with a warm roll and two fresh muffins. With Aggie sniffing everything in sight, Elizabeth set off at a fast pace. She walked through the formal gardens, which were a lot less formal than they used to be and had grown to be ten times more beautiful through the years, and arrived at the grove that she enjoyed walking in on her prior visits.

She walked until she found the almost hidden path to the glade. There was no wind, so there was nary a ripple on the surface of the pond. The little bit of disturbance was caused by the odd fish breakfasting on the insects on the water's surface. The pond looked like a large mirror reflecting the surrounding trees and the sky above with the streaks of light produced by the rising sun.

Elizabeth sat on a big rock with Aggie looking at her expectantly and wagging her big tail. Johns was standing a little way off, but where he could see his charge and the area around her clearly. "I know what you want, Aggie," Elizabeth told her faithful friend who was getting on in years but was still as she always was. The tail began to thump the rock hard. Elizabeth broke the roll in half, popped one half into her mouth and offered the other half to Aggie who after one chew, swallowed it.

Next, she took the two muffins out of the cloth that the cook had wrapped them in. She called Johns over and gave him one and then ate the other herself. When she and Johns had finished the treats, Elizabeth returned to the grove and walked until she arrived at the parsonage. Mrs Bamber was out collecting eggs and waved to Elizabeth.

"What a big dog Aggie is, Lady Elizabeth. Each year I see her, I marvel at her size. It is a pity that my boys are yet abed, they would love to pet her," the kindly woman said.

"You may tell your sons that when we ride this afternoon, I will come by with Aggie for them to spoil," Elizabeth offered.

"That is very kind of you to indulge them, my Lady," Mrs Bamber stated. Each gave a slight curtsey and Elizabeth continued her ramble across the park, heading back towards the house.

~~~~~~~/~~~~~~~

The next note pleased Mrs Fitzpatrick no end.

Return end of April. Feeling safe, will start discharging outriders. By next spring, down to two per carriage.

It meant another year to wait, but if it meant that their guard would be down, it was worth it. Finally, she would be able to execute her plan! She would not inform her pet Wickham yet; she would wait until they were much closer to the date of execution before she did that. She knew from his actions at Pemberley all those years ago that he was impulsive, so she would not allow him to spoil her plans a second time. If she even suspected that he would be an impediment this time, she would simply have him killed.

Wickham was no closer to devising a plan to get the old lady to withdraw a significant sum from the bank. As far as he knew, all of her money was in one bank, unaware that she used three. The one he knew of was the one that sent her supposed 'quarterly widow's pension', which had to be a fortune.

He resigned himself to the fact that he would not be able to extract money from the old bat, so what would he do? Then he had an epiphany. After he killed the one he hated, he would kidnap Georgiana Darcy! She would be older now and would fetch
~~~~~~~

him a handsome ransom. He was certain that her dowry would be above twenty thousand pounds, so he would demand that sum, which was more than enough for him to make his way to the former colonies and a new start. If he happened to take her virtue before returning her, so much the better! Better still, if she was with child, he would have a right to the Darcy fortune when his heir was born!

~~~~~~~/~~~~~~~

Jones hoped that his secret employer would not be angry with him, as he still did not have any significant news for her. So far, there had been no summons to meet with his 'brother' so it seemed like he had not fallen out of favour. He was sure that he had Branch in his confidence to the point where he would soon be able to share his true reason for being at Pemberley with him and gain him as an accomplice. He would be able to glean much better intelligence on the movements of the families that his employer craved.

Branch had been making sure that whoever was paying for the information was continuing to receiving little titbits to whet the appetite. The master had planned that they would appear practically unguarded in about a year. He had said that the person he suspected to be behind Jones was not the most patient of people, so he was deriving pleasure from dragging out the time of the eventual confrontation.

The aim was to catch all of the criminals in one fell swoop; that way there would be no stragglers or loose ends to deal with at a later date. The master, his son, the Earl, and the Lieutenant-Colonel were working on a very detailed plan that would have the perpetrators think they had an easy target, until the trap was sprung.

~~~~~~~/~~~~~~~

Will Darcy was enjoying a quiet Easter with the Bingleys and Hursts. There were visits from friends in the neighbourhood, but with one more month of deep mourning left for Bingley and Mrs Hurst, the celebration of the Lord's resurrection was subdued.

Bingley had taken to estate management with gusto, and combined with his new resolute personality, Will was confident that it would not be too many more months before he would be able to leave his friend to it with a clear conscience.

Will missed being with his family for Easter—especially Elizabeth. He knew the De Melvilles were part of the group at Rosings, but he was heartened when he remembered what his parents had told him about their observations of the interactions between Wes and Lizzy.

He knew that he needed her in his life like he needed the air to breathe. She was essential to his happiness, and he was starting to believe that it was not just from his side. He did not want to be presumptuous, but he had done as his parents suggested and during the days at Pemberley before his return south, he had surreptitiously observed her and she did seem to look at him a lot, and he saw no disapprobation as she did.

Will had gone into Meryton to the bookseller, whose store he frequented at least once a week, and was always welcomed warmly by the proprietor. He purchased a calendar for both the current and the following year. He had circled the first day of February 1798 as the possible date of his cousin's come out and had taken to crossing off each day as it passed. He willed time to speed up as he was impatient for the day that he would be able to dance with her at her coming-out ball.

~~~~~~~/~~~~~~~

One afternoon the weather had decided that some spring rain was in order, so a group was sitting in one of the drawing rooms. The younger group of Alex, Lily Gardiner, and the twins were off playing some games in another parlour. The parents were all enjoying a quiet discussion in the smaller drawing room.

Anne and Ian had shared how much they had enjoyed their honeymoon at Seaview Cottage. Once they were done, Jane and Perry described the enjoyment that they had in seeing so many varied locations, noting that they had followed the same path that Perry and Andrew had taken on their grand tour, making
~~~~~~~

brief stops around the Mediterranean. The big deviation from the grand tour was from the Kingdom of Sicily they had to cross the sea to the Sultanate of Egypt.

They described the ride on the animal known as the ship of the desert, a camel, and how they had looked on the great pyramids at Giza, and seen the enigmatic looking sphinx with her missing nose. Jane had told the listeners that she could not imagine how the pyramids had been constructed, as when they got close enough the sheer size of the stone blocks that were used had astounded her.

Luckily there were not too many days of rain, so there were many outdoor activities. Wes De Melville was beginning to get the idea that Elizabeth did not think of him as any more than her friend's brother. He had asked Retta to try and find out what Elizabeth's feelings were, but she had flatly and correctly refused his application. He was not willing to give up yet. He would bide his time until she came out into society and then he would present his suit because life with her would be truly pleasant.

Elizabeth was wishing that it was two years in the future, and she had been presented and already had a suitor, though it was definitely not Lord Wesley De Melville. She was not yet aware that her brother Andrew had agreed to share the privilege of approving her suitors with her birth father.

When Andrew had approached him a few days before about the subject, Bennet had been touched, Andrew would propose that he have a role in approving or disapproving of any suitors for Elizabeth. It was not something that Bennet had been expecting, but it was an office that he was very pleased to be able to fulfil when the time came.

Like most in the family, Bennet had noted that Elizabeth had two potential suitors before she had even taken her curtsy before the queen. And he, like most everyone else, was aware of her obvious preference for her cousin Darcy. He would be interested to see if the two would be able to get out of their own way and become a couple.

Tammy had never seen her husband happier. When they had

first reunited with Lizzy, she had feared that there might be tension between the adoptive and birth families, but her worries had been for naught. The families had integrated so well it was like they had always been one large family. Lizzy had started calling her Mother Tammy some months after she publicly added the title of 'Father' to Bennet. She understood the delay and would have been happy to continue on as Aunt Tammy, but her heart had swelled with happiness the first time Elizabeth had used the appellation.

The De Melvilles and the Ashbys departed for Surrey a week after Easter. Elizabeth and Georgiana felt bereft of Retta's and especially Amy's company after the latter had been with them for many months, though they were not allowed to wallow in their sorrow as they had the Bennets and Rhys-Davies with them yet.

Towards the end of April, the Bennets, Fitzwilliams, Rhys-Davies, and Darcys took their leave of Anne and Ian. The Bennets went to Hertfordshire and the other three families travelled north. It was the very day that a joyous Marie informed her husband that she had missed her courses for two consecutive months.

CHAPTER 13

June 1797

Will was finally home after he had completed his duty to his friend Charles Bingley. Elizabeth was looking forward to them establishing their prior routine of meeting once or twice a week to discuss a book, politics, or anything else that grabbed their attention.

It was getting close to the first celebration of her joining the family that was not celebrated as her birthday. To differentiate it from her actual birthday, Marie and her mama had planned a family celebration without chocolate cake. There would be a festive meal at Snowhaven, followed by an array of Elizabeth's other favourite desserts, which would include a chocolate pudding to placate any disappointment Elizabeth may have at not having her favourite cake served.

Although she was looking forward to the celebration with glee, Elizabeth felt a tinge of sadness. She had noticed recently that Aggie had started to slow down. She was approaching her eighth year, and as much as she did not want to think about it, she remembered her father explaining to her before she chose Aggie that large dogs like Great Danes seldom lived past the age of ten. Though in truth, all knew Aggie had chosen her. Being prepared was helpful, but it would not make it any less sad when that day eventually arrived.

There had been an extremely good piece of news shared a sennight before. Elizabeth thought back to that afternoon and the pleasurable thoughts drove the maudlin ones about Aggie's mortality to the recesses of her mind, for now.

Andrew and Marie had requested that their mother and Lizzy join them in their private sitting room. Marie, who was glowing with happiness, nodded to Andrew. "This morning Marie felt the quickening. We had suspected for some time that Marie is with child, but we wanted to wait to make an announcement until it was felt."

"How can you have a family meeting without me?" came from the doorway, where Richard stood in his regimentals.

"Itch!" Elizabeth exclaimed and launched herself at her brother, who she had not seen for months. Even at sixteen, she welcomed Richard in the same boisterous manner that she had for many years.

"Andrew!" admonished his mother, "did you omit to tell us that your brother would be home today, or at all?"

"It may have slipped my mind, mother," Andrew hedged, sporting a big grin and happy he had surprised his mother and Lizzy.

"I told Andrew he should have informed you two, but you know how my husband likes surprises," Marie smiled at the man who she loved.

"It sounds like I am to be an uncle, sister; did I hear correctly?" Richard smiled at his newest sister.

"Yes, Itch, you did hear what Marie said, for I am to be an aunt!" Elizabeth answered happily.

"And that will give me the title of grandmother," Elaine sighed. She was overjoyed at the news, but there was a touch of sadness that her beloved Reggie was not there to share in the wonder of their first grandchild, who would possibly be the new Lord Hilldale. Richard saw the look on his mother's face and hugged her.

"Papa would have loved to be a grandfather," he agreed softly next to her ear. Elaine was choked up so could not answer, just nodded her head as she hugged him in return.

"Has your state been confirmed, Marie?" Elizabeth asked.

"Yes, Dr. Gravelle saw me after we returned from Rosings. It was confirmed then, and he agreed all was going well. Before you ask, I sent an express to Longview Meadows just before Andrew and I requested that you join us."

Elizabeth was snapped out of her reverie as she heard the sound of carriages on the drive. She made her way towards the entrance with all speed as Jane, Perry, and Aunt Rose had just arrived.

~~~~~~~~/~~~~~~~~

Jones had taken Branch into his confidence a few weeks earlier. He had explained that he was just reporting some benign movements of the family to one who had enlisted his help and was hoping to have an 'unintentional' meeting and present an investment opportunity. Branch had played the part very well, acting as if this was the first time he was made aware of Jones' additional employment. Branch had agreed to provide him the 'harmless' information about the family's travel plans and had convinced Jones to allow him to carry the fortnightly notes to place in the hiding place in the chestnut tree on the green at Kympton.

After what Jones believed was Branch's first task in his plan, he quizzed him to make sure that he had placed the note as he had instructed and returned the cover to its place to hide the knothole. Once Jones was satisfied, he relaxed and was pleased that he was saved from having to ride all the way there and back when he was running out of excuses and that he had an ally who would help for less than one-third of what he was being paid for the job.

~~~~~~~~/~~~~~~~~

Mrs Fitzpatrick's anticipation was beginning to build. She could not grab the newest note from her secret spy fast enough when the footman delivered it.

One quarter of the out riders now discharged. No major travel until next Easter. Family not going to Rosings but lake district. Will notify once the route is decided.

Her mouth started to water. This was it. In less than nine months she would show them all. She decided that it was time to start recruiting those whose silence could be bought regardless of the activities they did. She estimated, based on the fact that by then there would only be two outriders per carriage, that she would need twenty men to whom she would offer one hundred pounds each. She smiled to herself. She would save one hundred pounds by paying one less and sending Wickham as part of the group.

The road from either Pemberley or Snowhaven to the lakes was rarely travelled, and she knew the ideal spot. About ten miles past the point where the roads from the two estates met, it entered a heavily wooded forest and there was a bend where the road ahead was invisible. She would have her men block the path there and then take the carriages. It would look like a highwaymen holdup gone wrong when the bodies were discovered. In addition to their pay, she would allow the men to take anything of value from the bodies and coaches.

She would insist that the plan be carried out exactly as she devised and she would be there to see the looks on their faces just before they died as they discovered just how far superior she was to them. For the first time in many years, the former Lady Catherine de Bourgh laughed, although to anyone hearing her it sounded far more like a cackle.

George Wickham was sitting in his windowless room thinking about his plan to kidnap Georgiana Darcy. It hit him that if the old bat had them all killed, which he suspected was her plan, there would be no one to ransom Georgiana back to.

That was when he realized the full scope of all that implied. She would be heir to all of the Darcy estates! He would steal her away to Gretna Green and force her to marry him, and then it would *ALL* be his. It would be his ultimate revenge—to rule Pemberley and live like his mother had always told him was his due. Like his patroness, Wickham conveniently ignored or forgot that he was a wanted murderer who would hang as soon as he was arrested. He did not know it, but he had been found guilty in abstention and had the sentence of death waiting for him.

~~~~~~~/~~~~~~~

The Bennets had been invited to Snowhaven for the celebration on the twentieth of June, but had demurred. They decided that they would feel out of place celebrating the day that Lizzy was found by the Fitzwilliams. They were beyond grateful that she was, but the day represented sadness for them as much as it was a happy day for the Fitzwilliams.
~~~~~~~

William and John, who had not been able to visit the area because of their attendance at their respective schools, had been invited and accepted and arrived at the end of May. Letters were carried between Hertfordshire and Derbyshire almost weekly, as correspondence was now more inclusive than just moves for chess. Even though it was a rare time indeed for his daughter to lose to him, Bennet and Lizzy kept playing their games by courier.

The Gardiners would have been with them except that Maddie had presented her husband with an heir whom they named Edward Junior on the second day of May. He would, however, be called Eddie. It was hard for Bennet to believe, but his James would be off to Eton in August. That would only leave one son at home for just another year when Tom would follow his brother to school.

Both boys had learnt from tutors and masters as their older brothers had before them and were well prepared for school, hence Bennet's decision to start them at thirteen and not fourteen, like many others. At almost twelve, Kitty was turning into a very accomplished young lady. She had a very good soprano voice and played the pianoforte very well, but her passion was drawing and painting. She had a natural talent for art that had been vastly enhanced by the art master Bennet had engaged. Miss Jones, the long-time governess for the Bennets, had taught Kitty well, and she was on her way to being prepared for her to come out

Bennet told himself that it was at least six years distant. The Bennets would join the rest of the family from the north in Town for the little season. It would be the first time that they would all be back in town since the true connection between themselves and Lady Elizabeth Fitzwilliam had been revealed, so there was an expectation of much scrutiny by the Ton.

The last part was that which Bennet dreaded, but he knew that he would need to grin and bear it.

~~~~~~~/~~~~~~~

Charles Bingley and the Hursts had been in half-mourning
~~~~~~~

since the six-month mark had passed. One of the first social calls that Charles Bingley made after he switched to half-mourning was to the Longs at Longmeadow. They shared a common border and Bingley needed to talk to his neighbour about broken fencing between their properties. When he was shown into the drawing room, he almost stopped short, but his innate good manners caught him before he made a spectacle of himself.

Mandy Long was no longer a little girl. She had blossomed into a very pretty young lady. With light brown hair and light green eyes, she was nothing like the blond-haired, blue-eyed, willowy ladies that had attracted Bingley before. She had a fuller figure, but everything was in proportion. Her younger sister Cara was transforming into a pretty girl as well. If memory served, Mandy would be sixteen in another month and be out in local society, just in time for the next assembly.

"Welcome, Mr, Bingley," his hostess said, snapping his thoughts from her older daughter. "Would you like some tea before you and my husband closet yourselves in the study?"

"Uhm...er...yes please, Mrs Long," Bingley recovered. It had been a while since he had felt tongue-tied. The mistress rang for tea and her daughters helped her serve it. Bingley almost dropped his cup and saucer when Mandy delivered it to him and their ungloved hands grazed one another. Charles Bingley knew that he had never reacted to any female in this way before, not even when he imagined himself in love with the former Jane Bennet, now Duchess of Bedford.

Not long after tea, the two men excused themselves. Once the study door was closed, Long turned to Bingley and simply said: "Not until she is seventeen!" They then proceeded with their business as if not a word had been said on the subject of his daughter.

~~~~~~~/~~~~~~~

One day after the two young men arrived at Snowhaven from school, they were sitting in one of the parlours with their sisters. "Do you like being a duchess, Jane?" John asked.

"So far it is not much different from just being Perry's wife,"
~~~~~~~

Jane replied. "When we all are in Town for the little season, I dare say then I will see a difference."

"You are a cousin to the Queen and her family now," William pointed out.

"True, but in a way, so are all of you as you are my brothers and sisters," Jane reminded him.

"I would be happy to be like Aunt Anne," Elizabeth offered.

"Do you mean married to a Darcy?" Jane teased.

"Jane, what...no...that is not what I mean," Elizabeth spluttered.

"So, you would not like to be my sister, Lizzy?" Georgiana teased as William and John grinned, the Bennet siblings watching their younger sister squirm.

"I was not saying *any* of that!" Came the indignant reply. "What I meant is I would not mind marrying an untitled man like Aunt Anne did, to be out of the scrutiny of the Ton while being the mistress of an estate without all the pressure." Elizabeth tried to extricate herself from the Gordian knot that she was busy tying.

"You mean like Pemberley?" William asked smoothly.

"Yes exactly, William!" Elizabeth did something she had not done for a very long time, she stamped her foot in frustration as it seemed every time she tried, rather than untying the knot, in her tongue, it seemed to get tighter.

"That will be enough teasing, Lizzy, from all of us," Jane told the group seriously.

"Yes, your Grace," chorused the three co-teasers while Elizabeth gave them a look of disbelief. She knew how she felt about Will, but she still had no clue of his feelings for her. That was the one puzzle that she truly needed to solve.

CHAPTER 14

July 1797

Charles Bingley had been waiting for the assembly in Meryton with great anticipation. He had used whatever excuses he could in the interim to visit Longmeadow, but as much as he wanted to, he could not entertain properly at home out of respect for his mother. He had wanted to request sets ahead of time of Miss Long, but when he mentioned that to her father, he had requested that Bingley wait until the evening of the assembly. He had added that as this was her first assembly out locally, he would not allow more than one dance with any individual man.

Bingley had been somewhat disappointed, but when he thought about it, he could understand that her father did not want her overwhelmed. The good thing was that Long had made that restriction for the first assembly only. After that, it would be up to his oldest daughter to make decisions about granting more than one dance to any particular man.

On the night of the dance, Bingley was one of the first to arrive, and he was warmly welcomed by Sir William Lucas as that man assumed his usual post of the host. He was discussing a farming issue with Franklin Lucas, who since his reformation, had become the pleasant young man all had known prior to his studying at Oxford. Bingley was mid-sentence when the Longs arrived. He saw Mr and Mrs Long enter, followed by Miss Long. He excused himself and was the first to greet the Longs after Sir William.

"Mr Long, Mrs Long, Miss Long," he intoned as he bowed to each in turn. "Miss Long, if your first set is available, may I have the honour of the dance?" he asked hopefully. Miss Long looked to her parents, and her mother gave a slight nod.

"Thank you, Mr Bingley, all my sets are open so I would be honoured to dance the first with you," she agreed shyly.

"In that case, Mandy, I will claim the final set with you," her father stated, a sly wink at Bingley telling him that he was willing to help him claim his daughter's affections, if that was what she wanted by, taking the second most important dance as his own.

By the time the first set began, most of Miss Long's sets were claimed. In Meryton, where they were always more ladies than men at an assembly, it was rare that a lady did not sit out at least one set.

When the music commenced for the quadrille which was the first dance of the set, Charles was most pleased that his partner was such an accomplished dancer. Even though he had matured a lot since his father passed, some things were the same, he was still an affable young man who loved to dance. They passed the set very pleasantly talking about inconsequential things. At the end of the half-hour, which had passed too quickly for Bingley's liking, he led Miss Long back to her parents, bowing to her as he thanked her for the dance.

He did not know if she would be the one that he would marry yet, but he knew that he wanted to find out. He had given Mr Long his word that if his interest did reach that level, that he would not declare himself until after she was seventeen. Her father had shared that his daughters would not have a London season, despite Jane's offer to sponsor them. It was too much of an expense for him to justify with his income, and he would not allow *anyone* else to pay for it while his daughters remained at home under his protection.

Franklin Lucas danced the fourth set with Miss Long. He thought that she was pretty but felt no attraction to her besides that of a friend of the family. He picked up that Bingley's attention was tending toward the tender and had grown enough not to start a competition for the lady as there had been over Jane

Bennet. Other than wealth, the fact that he had been competing for her affections with another had given him a rush and stoked his competitive juices. It had been about his desires only; what Jane wanted had never been a factor in that equation. He had also noticed that the gaze she looked at Bingley with was brighter than the one she turned on him and hoped that he would one day see them happy as they deserved.

Since he had had his attitude adjusted by the good Colonel, he was a much happier person. He had eschewed confronting his tormentors from Oxford, not because he was afraid, but he simply decided that they were not worth his time and effort. He had moved on. And anytime he was tempted to stray off the righteous path, which was almost never, all he had to do was look in the mirror at the two teeth that had been bought to replace the two that had been justifiably knocked out his mouth.

Martha Bingley was being kept company by her mother, the Hursts, and the Bennets. With no young men or ladies at home to attend, Thomas and Tammy Bennet had accepted an invitation to visit with their neighbours. Bennet and Hurst were seated in the corner locked in an even battle of chess. Like his opponent, Hurst had been roundly beaten in the games that he played against Lady Elizabeth while she had been in the neighbourhood.

"How is the board's work progressing?" Martha asked. Tammy noted the progress as this was the first time that her friend had made such an inquiry since her husband's sudden death.

"We have had an abundance of funds since Jane donated her dowry to the foundation and then the Darcy, Rhys-Davies, and Fitzwilliams each matched the amount so we have more than we will ever need," Tammy explained. "In fact, we have so much funding that we are thinking of looking at another location in our shire, even possibly adding ones in Buckinghamshire, Bedfordshire, or Middlesex. We will be deciding the next location at our meeting next month."

"I would like to return to the committee," Martha offered.

"You know you are welcome, Martha, but are you ready to do that?" Tammy enquired.

"I believe that I am, and as it is not a social event or a celebration, I will not be dishonouring my Oscar. In fact, I believe he would be pleased as he supported the committee's work wholeheartedly." Martha was steadfast in her decision. Her mother and Louisa had both encouraged her to do so and were happy that she was ready to start living again, even in small measure.

~~~~~~~~/~~~~~~~~

Things were moving in the direction that she had deemed they should. The last note that Mrs Fitzpatrick had received was to let her know that another quarter of the outriders had been let go. They were on schedule to whittle down to two per vehicle by March, when the families were to depart for the Lake District.

According to her spy, they would meet at Pemberley and travel from there. He would have the departure date by Twelfth Night and she soon after, allowing her to finalise her plan which was sure to yield the results that she desired.

She too had decided to not give Wickham the facts about the operation until a week before. She had found a brigand by the names of Jamie McLamb. He would do anything for money, and he had nine other men, he was sure would work with him, and that they would know other nine who would do almost anything for one hundred pounds. As the leader, he had demanded two hundred pounds and it was something that she understood. It took a lot to lead people by their noses, so she had put up an argument for argument's sake, but in the end had agreed.

She would pay each man a quarter of his due before the job, the rest once it was completed to her liking. She was adamant that her plan would be followed to the letter or there would be no payment. McLamb had agreed to the stipulation—it was her money after all.

Wickham knew that the old bat was meeting with a man he had never seen before, but he could learn nothing about it. Ever since Hodges had almost given him a permanent smile, he had been very wary about questioning any of her men too closely. He
~~~~~~~~

knew that a footman was away for three days every fortnight, but there too he had no clue why or where he was going.

He was already spending the vast fortune that would be his once he married that little brat Georgiana Darcy. Once he had Pemberley, if she was not pleasing to him, he would just get rid of her and take another more willing wife. He would be able to play in any game of chance, regardless of the limit on wagering, or lack thereof. The dream of finally fulfilling his and his mother's dreams let him sleep better than he had since he had been forced to live with the old woman in Packwood.

~~~~~~~~/~~~~~~~~

Jones believed that he was controlling Branch when the opposite was true. There were four disguised guards in addition to Branch tasked with keeping an eye on Jones. Even when he slept, secure in the knowledge that his secret was safe, there was a man watching. As Branch carried and placed all of the missives for Jones, he was able to keep feeding Jones' employer whatever information the master wanted known.

If Jones' 'brother' sent a message to see him again, Jones would be incapacitated and Branch would take the meeting and be able to prove with ease that he was working with Jones. So far, the employer must have been happy with what was being received because other than retrieving the notes, the man had not requested a meeting with Jones again.

George, and Will Darcy and the Fitzwilliam brothers had a solid plan in place. As Richard trained men in military tactics, he was the one that planned the tactics which would be used to capture whoever was sent to cause mischief. On a weekend that he had been off, Richard and Will had ridden the way that they would take to the lake district from Pemberley.

They both agreed that the perfect place for an ambush would be the little clearing in the forest where the road took a sharp turn to the right. If it was their former Aunt planning the attack, it made sense that she would choose this location, as she had travelled the road many times over the years when she was still at Snowhaven.
~~~~~~~~

Everyone agreed that they would finalise the plan after Twelfth Night when the remaining information that their enemy required would be released. If it was Lady Catherine behind whatever was going to be attempted, the fact that she was Lady Anne's sister would count for nothing, and she would be handed over to the law. If there was a scandal it, now would be minor. The fact that Catherine de Bourgh was wanted for murder and had been disowned by all of her family, was well known among the Ton.

~~~~~~~~/~~~~~~~~

Like their father before them, the first time that William and John visited Pemberley they were awestruck by the Darcy library. William lost himself in the religious tracts, making no time for the anti-woman writings of Reverend Fordyce. John Manning spent many hours reading books, ancient and current, on the law.

The two Bennet sons would remain in Derbyshire until the end of June, then travel south to join the family. It was the first time that they had so much dedicated time to spend with their sister and both were amazed at her intellectual abilities. For a minute William wondered if he would be able to win such a woman, but he was not blind. He saw the way that the Darcy heir looked at his younger sister and how she looked at him. He had noticed something the first time they had all been together, but he had believed it to be only cousinly affection; something that he was now sure was not true.

As a surprise for Lizzy, a few days before the celebration, Anne and Ian Ashby arrived with their sister Amy accompanying them. Both Elizabeth and Georgiana were extremely happy to see their friend. Anne Darcy, knowing that Anne and Ian were coming and bringing Amy with them, had allowed her daughter to stay at Snowhaven for the rest of the summer, if she so desired, which of course she did.

"Anne, Ian, Amy! Why did you not inform us that you were travelling to see us?" Elizabeth asked.

"Because silly," Amy shot back and then giggled, "that would
~~~~~~~~

not be much of a surprise now, would it?"

"You and Georgie were the only ones who did not know," Marie, informed her younger sister with a smile.

"As it is a good surprise, I will not be vexed," Elizabeth teased back. Aggie, who had been sunning herself on the top step next to the front doors, gave a deep woof of welcome.

"It is good to see you too girl," Anne Ashby walked up the stairs to scratch Aggie's chest. The huge dog promptly rolled on her side to expose more of it and one hind leg made a scratching motion reflexively. When Anne ceased her ministrations, Aggie gave her a baleful look that asked why she stopped, but after no more scratches were forthcoming, she was soon snoring again.

Before they could enter the house, another surprise arrived in the form of Richard riding his horse. The yell of "Itch" rang in the air as Elizabeth spied her brother. She threw herself into his waiting arms. Knowing that her brother was tired from his long ride, Elizabeth released her grip on his neck, and after he greeted the rest of the family, he took himself to his chambers, but not before asking Mrs Smythe to send up hot water for him.

The following evening the family had the festive meal to celebrate Elizabeth's discovery and arrival at Snowhaven. As would be expected, the celebration was enjoyed by all. There was no separation of the sexes that night, and each of the ladies entertained the family, either alone or in duets. Elizabeth and Jane had practised a piece for the harp and pianoforte which they played. They also sang a song where Jane's mezzo soprano blended perfectly with Elizabeth's contralto. As she usually did, Elizabeth performed an Italian aria to end the evening.

Will sat mesmerised as he listened to the lady who he loved sing like an angel. At the very least, he had crossed more days off his calendar. A little more than one- and one-half years to go until Elizabeth had her come out. He would not be able to declare himself immediately, but he, who did not love dancing in a crowded ball room would make a statement that would be hard to misinterpret by the number of times he wanted to dance with his cousin, if she would allow it.

Before they all left for their chambers at the end of the evening, Andrew informed them that he and Uncle George would like to speak to the family on the morrow. It was agreed to meet at ten once everyone was done with breaking their fasts.

Before ten, all of the family was assembled in the family sitting room. Andrew and Uncle George, with a little input from Richard and William, informed all of them about the ongoing espionage at Pemberley and what was being done to thwart whatever nefarious plans were being made.

Richard explained that they planned to capture all involved at one time so that they would not have to go chasing conspirators all over the kingdom. "Is someone else trying to hurt me again?" Elizabeth asked. "I do not want anyone to get hurt because of me."

"As you well know it has never been 'because of you,' as these people will do what they do regardless. In this case, the harm is aimed at the Darcy and Fitzwilliam families as a whole. You never had the *pleasure* of meeting the former Lady Catherine de Bourgh, Lizzy, but we believe that she is behind this. We fear that she is insane." Richard went on to remind Lizzy how the mad woman had murdered a maid and then fled.

"I am sure that in her warped perception, my sister believes that somehow we are all responsible for her problems, and she is now trying to take her revenge. She was also obsessed with gaining Pemberley's fortune by any means she could devise," Lady Anne told all sadly.

"So you see, Sprite," Andrew gave her a hug, "this is not about you. We do suspect that Wickham has found sanctuary with her, so we hope to capture them all in one fell swoop."

"If that miscreant is there, I would like to have a little discussion with him," Richard growled malevolently. No one hearing him had any doubt that his 'talk' would be a message no words could deliver.

"We will not allow them to harm a hair on any of our loved ones' heads," Uncle George added resolutely.

After the discussion, it was agreed that everyone who wanted to ride would meet at the stables in a half hour. Andrew elected to stay with his wife in the company of his mother and mother-in-law as even the Darcy parents would be joining the ride. The four, who remained inside, discussed the upcoming little season and the family's first foray to London in a while. Andrew and Marie would not be on the trip as it would be too soon after Marie's confinement and too cold to travel with a new born.

Elizabeth would stay between Darcy and Bennet houses with Uncle George as her temporary guardian. Elaine would stay at Darcy House as there was no reason to open Matlock House just for her. Everyone would have to brace for the scrutiny of the Ton, although they hoped that, given the time that had passed it may have lessened somewhat, but none were confident of that.

CHAPTER 15

October/November 1797

In coordination with the Bennets, it had been decided that the Fitzwilliams, Rhys-Davies, and Darcys would arrive in town on the twelfth day of October. The Ashbys, both from Kent and Surrey, and the De Melvilles would also arrive close to that same date. There was no doubt that when the knocker at Bennet House was set, that there would be a deluge of ladies of the Ton who wanted to pay a morning call. But if they suspected that they would have a chance to ingratiate themselves with Mrs Bennet on her own, they would be sorely disappointed. The current plan was that they would walk into a room with duchesses, countesses, and some merely titled 'Lady' so anyone who thought that they could take advantage of the perceived naïveté of the mistress of the house, would be put in their place before they knew what was happening.

Elaine was torn between accompanying Elizabeth to town and staying home with the proud parents. On the eighth day of October, Marie had entered her final confinement, and after many hours a squalling, Lord Hilldale was born. He was named Reginald Sedgewick Fitzwilliam after his two grandpapas, neither of whom he would ever have the pleasure of knowing. Both Elaine and Rose were beyond pleased with the name Andrew and Marie chose, and both swore that they could see their late husbands in the new babe. No one contradicted them even though they all knew that it would be at least a year before one could see any such likenesses.

Little Lord Reggie, as his nursemaid had dubbed him, had a very powerful set of lungs, so when he was hungry or upset there were few at Snowhaven who were not aware of the fact. Marie elected to ignore the mores of the Ton and would feed her son herself; she felt that she bonded with him in ways that those who did not provide sustenance to their new-borns did not. She did agree to have a wet nurse hired for the night time feedings so that she could get restful a night's sleep and recover that much faster from the birth of her son.

Dr. Gravelle had been in the next room but was never needed, as the midwife had delivered the Fitzwilliam heir with no issues. He was bald when he was born, and rather than the deep blue Fitzwilliam's eyes, his had a touch of green in the blue that most babies are born with. Grandmother Rose informed them that both Perry and Marie had been born with the same colour eyes, then within weeks, theirs changed to the deep green colour they now had.

As much as both grandmothers hated to leave Marie a few days after her giving birth, knowing she was in no danger, and with Andrew and all of their fussing servants, she and the babe would be well taken care of, the two dowagers agreed to leave as scheduled.

Alex was one of the happiest in the family to learn that little Reggie had been born as he was tired of being the youngest even though he was a full ten years old. He happily resigned the title and passed it onto Reggie whether he wanted it or not. Alex was doing very well with his tutors and seemed to follow his father and brother with an affinity for the written word.

Being so close to the Dragoons training grounds, Richard would be able to see his family in Town a few times a week. Elaine and Elizabeth, in particular, were keen to see him again as they had not since his surprise visit to Snowhaven in June. Seeing her second son was one of the factors that tipped the scale for Elaine in her decision to go to Town rather than stay with her first grandson and his parents.

Although it was cold already in the north, Will and his father elected to ride alongside the carriages, at least part of the way. Aunt Anne, Elizabeth, Georgiana, and Alex rode in a coach which was more than large enough to accommodate them when they decided that they would like to be inside out of the elements. Luckily, Aggie was stretched out on a bench in one of the servant's conveyances, otherwise, there would not have been room for six.

Will decided to brave the cold for as long as he could, as he was aware that if he sat opposite the object of his love, he would stare at her, and he neither wanted her to think that he was looking to find fault as his father warned nor did he want to sit there looking like the besotted man he was. The fact that he did not ride inside all the times, that his father did harken the memory from years before when he had distanced himself from her. Elizabeth started to wonder if she had done something to displease him as he again did not seem to want to be in company with her as much as he used to. If she had been privy to his calendar as he crossed off each day, they got ever closer to her come out, there would have been no such questions in her mind.

~~~~~~~/~~~~~~~

Before Branch departed for town, he had arranged that Jones be one of the stable hands that would be sent to London to augment the Darcy House hands while the family was in residence. A note was left in the knothole by him before the departure so that Jones' employer would not be suspicious which would happen if the fortnightly reports ceased.

Jones trusted his good friend Branch completely with collaboration in gaining intelligence, but he had kept the name and location of his secret employer from Branch as he remembered her warning that she would see him dead if he ever divulged that information to anyone. Branch had asked once, and when Jones explained why he could not share that information Branch did not push or ask him again as he was sure that would raise suspicion.

The master had rejected Branch's suggestion that they lock Jones up since the notes were being written by himself and Jones was essentially superfluous. The master had decided that, out of an abundance caution, Jones would be seen doing his nor-
~~~~~~~

mal tasks just in case there was anyone they were not aware of watching.

~~~~~~~~/~~~~~~~

Mrs Fitzpatrick was annoyed that she would not receive any more notes until the critical one which would come once the families returned to Derbyshire after Twelfth Night. She begrudgingly agreed with the note as she did know that most families of the Ton, and the Darcys in particular, always sent additional servants to London when they were to be in residence for any length of time. She read her note again:

I am to London. Smaller house so will not be able to slip away unnoticed and no arrangement for Town drop-offs made. Will be back days after Twelfth Night. Have your man check a week after Twelfth Night. The next note will have the date and details requested.

She hated that not everything was by her will, but she accepted that trying to force some sort of communication while he was in London had the potential of spoiling all of her plans. She did dispatch one of her footmen to Town to ride past the mews at Darcy House to verify that Jones had been honest with her in saying he was in town. Five days later, the man returned and confirmed that he had seen Jones working in the stables. This for her confirmed all his missives as truth.

She met with McLamb fortnightly, not because there was any new information, but she loved to exert her will over all she paid to show them that they owed her deference while being beneath her notice. The plan was in place, all she needed now was the date.

Wickham had not been able to glean any information about the man that met with the old bat every fortnight. As he was frustrated in those efforts, he expended his time imagining how it would feel to have control of Pemberley. As soon as he was married to the Darcy girl, his first act would be to have Lady Catherine beaten to death with her own walking stick to repay her for all of the times that she had beaten him it.

He would get much pleasure taking the foundling's life, regardless of the fact that she was not a mongrel. How dare she
~~~~~~~~

be born higher than he! That meant Lady Catherine's demise was actually second on his list, and then remembered she was not Lady anything. The crown had rescinded her honorific title some years back. At the time she had raged against her family and added the offence to the long list that she already held against them. It amused him how much she hated losing an appellation she could no longer use because of her assumed identity.

The only thing he did know was that whatever was being planned, it would happen in the new year. He was down to months of waiting left; after the years spent biding his time, what was a few more months?

~~~~~~~~/~~~~~~~~

As life tends to do, it moves on and in September, Louisa brought Harold Oscar Hurst into the world. He would be known as Harry, named for his two grandfathers, one live and one deceased, and was the source of much joy for his parents, grandparents, great-grandmother, and various uncles and aunts. It was especially good news for the Hursts whose entailed estate would now remain in the hands of a Hurst beyond the younger Mr Harold Hurst.

Little Harry, at six weeks old, had a tuft of light brown hair and his eyes were now light brown like his father's. Mary was enamoured with her new role of big sister, even if she had preferred that her mama gift her with a sister. As her parents had explained, they could not exchange Harry for a sister and he would have to do.

For Martha, it was the final push that she needed to embrace her upcoming change to half-mourning. Nothing would replace her Oscar, but having Mary and now little Harry in the house to keep her busy when she was not occupied with the committee and their work was a pleasure. Each day she felt a little more resigned to her status as a widow, and with the new life in her house, she saw that she had many reasons to embrace living. She admitted to herself that her Oscar would have wanted her to carry on and not stop as she had for a time.
~~~~~~~~

Charles Bingley was looking forward to the little season where he would see his friends again as he was about to end his period of half-mourning. He had ordered the house on Gracechurch Street to be opened for the first time since his late father had passed away in the study there almost a year before.

He was looking forward to society, but he was not looking for a lady any longer. He was in love with Miss Amanda Long. He and Mandy had not made any declarations one to the other, but unless he was blind and could not read signals, he was sure that she had a tender regard for him as well. She would be seventeen at the end of June of the coming year, and one month after that he had permission from Mr Long to declare himself. He knew that three and twenty was relatively young to settle down and marry for a man, but why wait once you have found the one that you love?

~~~~~~~/~~~~~~~

The Bennets arrived at Bennet House within hours of the Derbyshire and Yorkshire families arriving at their houses in Town. Perry, Jane, and Lady Rose would reside at his townhouse on St. James Square. It was the closest to Grosvenor Square of all of his properties in Town. Elizabeth would be at Darcy House until the end of October, then she would spend a fortnight at Bennet House, followed by a sennight at Birchington House with her sister Jane.

At each of their townhouses, there was an invitation from the King and Queen inviting them to Buckingham House for tea five days hence. It was not an invitation that one could refuse. The Bennets being included in the invitation was a further indication to the Ton of the royal support that they enjoyed. King George III had endured a very serious illness almost ten years earlier and there had been great concern for the monarch, but other than some eccentric behaviour, he seemed well again.

That night, the four arriving families met at Bennet House for a dinner where they were joined by the Gardiners and Phillips, who were staying with their in-laws. The dinner was loud, and the Bennet House's new cook showed off her abilities that
~~~~~~~

were enjoyed by all of the diners. In fact, the repast was so good that George Darcy joked with Bennet by offering him some first editions to be able to hire the cook away from Bennet House. Richard, who had arrived just before dinner, extoled the quality of the food over the swill that he was forced to eat in the army. No one felt sympathy for him as he did not look like he missed too many meals.

The ladies had an appointment at Madam Chambourg's modiste shop on Bond Street in the morning to which Lady Elaine would accompany her daughter. The plan was to meet up with the men at Gunter's after the modiste. Bennet and the Darcy men would spend the morning browsing the books at Hatchard's, and by browsing, all three meant purchasing. They would meet Perry at the club, and then the four of them would make for Gunter's.

As Elizabeth had grown both in height and shape since she had last visited Madame Chambourg's, she was measured again, as was Georgiana who was already taller than Elizabeth. It was Tammy and Kitty Bennet's first time, so full measurements for them were also taken. Jane and Anne Ashby were both clients and their wedding gowns were Madame Chambourg creations, so they only needed to look at the sketches and plates that were on display. Ladies Anne and Rose decided not to order anything as they both had orders being worked on that were requested before arriving in Town.

Elizabeth felt that shopping was a necessary evil. She would have preferred to be outdoors, either riding Saturn or taking Aggie for a walk in Hyde Park rather than leaving it to one of the footmen. The ordeal was thankfully over after her mother had ordered a half dozen gowns and day dresses for her daughter which were appropriate for one on the cusp of coming out into society.

Anne returned to De Bourgh house with her husband directly from the visit to the modiste as she was feeling rather fatigued. They also had things they needed to do—one of which was to rename the house, Ashby House.

~~~~~~~~/~~~~~~~~

After the visit to Hatchard's, the men headed to White's to meet up with Perry. He had previously made an appointment at his solicitor's office so he had missed the chance to visit the book shop with his friends. The three men were shown to a private alcove where Perry waited for them. As they walked towards the alcove, there were not a few men who tried to work out who the unknown greying gentleman in their party was. It was not long before word got around that he was none other than Thomas Bennet, Lady Elizabeth Fitzwilliam's birth father.

Much to Bennet's relief, they did not stay long, and although the three greeted one or two acquaintances briefly, they were moving too fast for anyone to request an introduction to him. After retrieving their outerwear and canes from an attendant, the four struck out towards Gunter's.

The ladies had been waiting for some minutes when Ladies Rose, Anne, and Elaine saw a good friend of theirs on the opposite side of the shop and went to talk to her. Only Jane, Elizabeth, and Georgiana remained at the table.

Sitting in the corner with two friends was a Miss Theodora Price. She had come out the past season and there had been no interest in her. The family was aware that she had been heard to boast how she would be the next Mrs Darcy. Her father was a tradesman, but that is not why she was universally disliked. She was cut from the same cloth as the late Caroline Bingley who believed that she should be higher in society than she was, so she acted as if it were so. She had not seen her quarry in Town for more than a year, and had long been in a snit that the Darcys had not responded to the invitation to her coming out ball.

Despite all her training, she had ignored the unwritten rule that one did not send an invitation to those to whom one had never been introduced. She had heard that the family stayed away from London because of Lady Elizabeth Fitzwilliam's family situation, and in her narrow mind, it was that lady's fault that she did not have three sets at her ball with the Darcy heir. When she saw the matrons leave the table and that Lady Elizabeth was
~~~~~~~~

sitting there with two unknown blondes, she decided that it was time to make her displeasure known so that the *lady* would not make the same mistake again.

"They let just anyone in here," she sneered as she flounced up to the table where the three family members sat in conversation. "Foundlings should be in a workhouse, not here with us members of the first circles."

Elizabeth saw her mother, Mother Bennet, and Aunt Anne, start to move towards her, as did Biggs from his position in the corner. She shook her head very slightly, telling them to hold their positions and that she wanted to handle this.

"Mores of society dictate that we should be introduced before you address me, as you have broken them already, who are you to address me thusly?" Elizabeth asked acerbically.

"I am Miss Theodora Price," the woman returned trying to affect as much hauteur as she could.

"You are a member of the first circles, Miss Price?" She turned to Jane with a big smile and wink, unseen by Miss Price and her two friends. "I have heard of you and as far as I know, you are a tradesman's daughter. Did the rules change, Jane?" She asked as she saw that the four men had arrived and were watching her performance with her mothers and aunt.

"What does that insipid nobody who apparently smiles too much know of the *first* circles?" Miss Price spat out, her words dripping with disdain. She thought that the gasps she heard were sounds of agreement and so did not check herself nor her surroundings as it was high time someone put this one in her place. "Wait until my friends, the Darcys hear how you dared speak to me so!"

Elizabeth looked past the homely woman. "Let us ask them, should we not? Uncle George, Aunt Anne?" she said their names without raising her voice because it was so quiet everyone present would hear her doing so. She then looked at the unknown blonde to her left, "Cousin Georgiana, what have you to say about your *friend* Miss Price?"

Miss Price and her friends, who had been certain they were in control of the situation, now looked positively green around the gills. They had not known that Lady Elizabeth was here with her family; they had thought that the older blonde was her companion and the younger a friend of no consequence, but it was Miss Darcy!

"Lizzy, will you introduce this person to me?" Jane requested with ice in her voice.

"Certainly, Jane. This is Miss Theodora Price..." Miss Price seemed to find her voice and tried to salvage the mess that she had made.

"How dare you request that I, your better, be introduced to you?" She demanded; her haughty indignation evident in her voice. Again, there were many gasps, and now a low hum of whispers started in the background.

"As I was trying to say before your ignorant outburst, Miss Price, may I introduce *her Grace*, Lady Jane Rhys-Davies, the *Duchess* of Bedford." Elizabeth's smile spread as the colour drained from Miss Price's pallor.

"If I were all of you," Jane said her voice icy as she stood and glared at the three, "I would not try and show my face in society —ever again!"

Miss Price's cohorts fled the store, trying to distance themselves from the social suicide their friend was committing, but running would not help them. As if it could not get worse for Miss Price, she saw Lady Elizabeth smile as someone approached behind her.

"This gentleman," she indicated the man that had now walked over to stand behind the Duchess, "is my brother Perry, though to you he is *his Grace,* Lord Peregrine Rhys-Davies, *Duke* of Bedford!" The rest of their party now joined those seated. "Also joining us are my Uncle and Aunt, Mr George and Lady Anne Darcy, and my Cousin Fitzwilliam Darcy. Before I continue, Uncle and Aunt? Gigi does not seem to know her yet she claimed a friendship with your family. Do you know this harpy?"

"Until this day, we have never had the displeasure of meeting this person!" Lady Anne responded, her eyes ice cold as she turned her gaze on Miss Price. Nodding that she had expected as much, Elizabeth then stood and closed in on the young lady who was now shaking due to shock.

"If I were you, I would follow your friends and follow my sister's sage advice and run; run as far as you can as fast as you can, because after today the cut direct will be the *best* that you can expect to receive in polite society!" Elizabeth advised the upstart. With that, Miss Price turned and walked out as fast as she could, then took the Duchess and Lady Elizabeth's advice and ran.

~~~~~~~~/~~~~~~~~

As they had expected, over the next sennight, Bennet House was besieged by callers during visiting hours. Once word was spread of who Mrs Bennet's supportive friends were, any with nefarious plans gave up and kept away. By the end of the sennight the visits were at a manageable volume and Tammy had met a few ladies with whom it would not be a chore to get to know better.

The tea with the royals was a roaring success, especially as the King was in rare form—so much so that one would not have been able to detect that he had been so ill if they had not known so already. As always, it ended with musical performances. The Queen was charmed by Lady Elizabeth's solo performance; however, the highlight of the performance was the duet that the sisters played and their voices blended perfectly.

Towards the end of November, William and John arrived from Cambridge, and a few days after that James arrived from Eton. Before they realised it, the time to quit town and head home for Christmastide at Longbourn was upon them. On the eighteenth, the Monday before Christmas, many coaches were seen to depart for Hertfordshire.
~~~~~~~~

CHAPTER 16

December 1797/January 1798

As cold as it was, Jones was pleased to be returning to Pemberley. He and three other Pemberley stable hands were in an old carriage that Branch was driving. He had been told that the families would be returning to Derbyshire after Twelfth Night rather than return to Town for the season in order to prepare for a trip to the lakes for Easter.

When he had checked with Branch, his friend had confirmed that all members of the Darcy and Fitzwilliam families would be headed to the Fitzwilliams' property, Lake View House. Jones wanted a note placed in the tree as soon as they arrived back at the estate, but changed his mind when Branch reminded him that the note that they sent before their departure had said only to check the knothole after Twelfth Night, so there would be no point in placing the note.

A few days before the family headed to Hertfordshire for Christmastide, Branch was summoned to the kitchen. Killion, the Darcy House Butler, then led him to the master's study where he met with the master, his son, the nephew in the army, and the gentleman, Mr Bennet. He was informed that the date he would provide in his note was the second day of April, the Monday before the Easter weekend.

The men had given him leave to use his discretion on when and how to take Jones into custody, whether he felt the need to do so quietly once Branch and those travelling with him returned to Pemberley or at any time after. The master then had given him a missive for Mr Forester, the former officer in command of the guards and outriders at the Darcy estate.

As he drove the team north, Branch did not think there would be a reason to detain Jones before the first Monday in April, but he would keep his eyes open and arrest him if he felt it was needed.

~~~~~~~~/~~~~~~~

'This is the last Christmas those who disrespected me will have!' Mrs Fitzpatrick cackled to herself. *'It will all be mine soon, I will get everything I deserve, should always have had!'*

She had continued her fortnightly meetings with McLamb and was satisfied that her plan would be executed flawlessly. She had, after all, threatened him with the intent to not pay him if he did not do as she decreed, and it was not an idle threat as he would never be able to see that kind of money for a single day's action, she was certain she would soon have her due.

And McLamb had been correct, his nine men had easily recruited nine more who would have sold their souls for the one hundred pounds that they would earn. A more degenerate bunch she could not imagine! There was not a single conscience between them, and that exactly suited her purposes. She required men of no morals that would not balk at the disposal of women or children.

Just a day earlier she had told Wickham that he would finally be of use to her. Little did she know, Wickham was currently reviewing their conversation yet again.

"We will soon be moving against your old friends," she informed Wickham, looking uncommonly pleased with herself. "You will be told the details closer to the time, but your knowledge of the area around Pemberley will be valuable. I will be rid of all of them in one fell swoop!"

"When and where will this take place?" Wickham asked, hoping she would reveal at least some details.

"Closer to the time, I said. In the meanwhile, the man who will lead the operation for me may have questions about the area; if he does, you will answer anything he asks. Do not let me hear that you have tried to ask him any questions. Am I rightly understood?" she asked acerbically.
~~~~~~~~

"Yes, you are Mrs Fitzpatrick," was his sullen reply.

Finally, they were to move against his enemies, and in truth, he only cared about two things; that he got to kill the foundling himself, and that he could somehow spirit Miss Darcy away, alive. He was hoping to make his own arrangement with this McLamb character in which he would pay him a hefty sum for his assistance as soon as he married Georgiana Darcy.

~~~~~~~~/~~~~~~~~

It was a very merry Christmas at Longbourn in 1797. The house was overflowing with family and friends, and the normally quiet master of the house was celebrating as much as anyone. All the principal families in the area had accepted invitations to a Christmas Eve party that was held in the ballroom to accommodate all of the guests. Only the children ages three or younger were in the nursery. May Gardiner was very proud that at four, she just missed the cut-off to have to be in the nursery. Mary Hurst was not happy that she was on the wrong side of the cut-off.

Andrew, Marie, and little Reggie had arrived two days earlier. At close to three months of age and a very robust, healthy boy, his parents had decided that he could travel. On the way to Longbourn, they had stopped often, making sure to exchange the cool warming bricks for hot ones as much as needed, turning the two-day trip into three days of travel.

Lady Rose had been correct. Reggie had the deep green eyes of his mother and Uncle Perry, the same colour that his late grandfather Sed had. He and the five-month-old Hurst heir, Harry, garnered much attention, especially from proud grandparents and in Harry's case, a great-grandparent, along with aunts, uncles, and cousins.

Martha Bingley did not repine her decision to once again attend celebrations now that she was in half mourning. Now that Louisa was fully recovered from Harry's birth, Martha was feeling much happier. She had been very worried as Louisa had lost more blood than Mr Jones had been happy with and it had taken her almost three weeks to recover, but recover she had and by
~~~~~~~~

the end of October, she was back to her old self.

Mrs Beckett was slowing as she approached her eighth decade, as to be expected. Martha had planned with her brother and sisters that they would visit Netherfield in June, and then at the end of the month, they would all take a slow trip to Scarborough with their mother. She would spend time with them until the end of August when she and Charles would then travel to Yorkshire and bring mother back to her home at Netherfield before the cold of the north set in.

Jane had not missed the looks that passed between her friend Mandy and Charles Bingley. She invited Mandy to come sit with her, Louisa Hurst, and Charlotte Pierce in a corner that had two settees place to form an 'L.' "I could not but notice that our Mr Bingley seems to follow you with his eyes wherever you go, Mandy," Jane observed.

"We are friends," Mandy hedged, though she blushed from the roots of her hair to her neck.

"There are not too many 'just friends' that look at one another the way that you and Mr Bingley look at each other," Charlotte said it for her so that their friend would be at ease to know that she was understood. Then she turned to her best friend. "What do you know, Louisa? Do not tell me that your brother does not talk about our Mandy at home."

"He may have said something to me…in confidence," Louisa agreed.

"When will you be out, Mandy?" Jane enquired.

"Papa said I will come out fully after I turn seventeen, in June," Mandy shared.

"Has he said when someone, let us say, a certain man with a red tinge in his hair who lives at Netherfield, may declare himself?" Charlotte asked with a smile and Mandy nodded.

"If he pays you his addresses, would you welcome them?" Jane asked gently. Mandy just looked at her hands as her blush burned hotter.

"You know it is your duty to answer a duchess, do you not?" Charlotte teased.

"Mandy, no one will force a confidence," Jane told her as she took her hand in hers and patted it. "All I hope is that, whether it is Louisa's brother who wins your heart or another, you choose your mate for love, felicity, and respect. I can tell you from my experience of almost a year, that there is nothing better than such a marriage."

"I agree," both Louisa and Charlotte chorused at the same time.

"When there is news to tell, I promise you that you will be among the first to know," Mandy said as her blush started to slowly recede.

As Franklin Lucas was pouring himself a glass of punch, he noticed Lady Elizabeth heading for the punch bowl, and that she was unaccompanied. He did not miss her brothers and cousin Darcy watching intently, ready to jump into action if there was a need. He also did not miss the two enormous footmen that were watching her every move. He was about to vacate the area of the punchbowl when she addressed him directly.

"Would you mind pouring me a glass of Mother Bennet's punch please, Mr Lucas," she requested.

"I do not think that your family will approve of my talking to you, your Ladyship," he said with a bow.

"It is I who initiated the contact, and we all know that your behaviour since that time has been exemplary. Not only did you apologise, but your actions much more so than your words prove that you were sincere in your resolution to change your path. So, as I am not talking to the man that was, but rather the one that is, I feel comfortable making the request I did," Elizabeth explained to a very relieved man.

He did as she asked and bowed. "I wish you and your family merry Christmastide, Lady Elizabeth."

"And I wish you and your family the same," Elizabeth returned as she curtsied and returned with her drink to where her brothers and Will were standing. She did not miss how the three men relaxed now that they could see she was not ill at ease. She would never be friends with Franklin Lucas, but she would now count him as an acquaintance.

The following day, everyone was up at the crack of dawn to exchange gifts in the drawing room where the Bennets, for the first time, were trying the Prussian tradition that he had read about of having a tree in the corner of the room decorated with all manner of things with an angel on the top. The three, Tom, Kitty, and Alex, who tried so hard to prove that they were ready to leave the nursery, were no less excited to open their gifts than the three Gardiner children.

Bennet presented Lizzy with a miniature of her Grandmother Beth, her namesake, and a small portrait that included all of the current Bennet family. Jane gifted her sister a bracelet and ear-bobs that matched her cross that she had worn since before she was kidnapped. Elizabeth was vastly touched by their thoughtful gifts. She presented her birth father with a rare first edition that she knew he had been searching for which Uncle George and Will had assisted her in finding. The look on Father Bennet's face was gift enough. She presented Jane with a cross just like hers, except encrusted with sapphires and with the words *'For my angel 'Anie'* engraved on the back. The exchange of gifts between the three led to much hugging and not a few tears.

After the gifts, the family broke their fasts and then changed for church. Even though it was cold with a light dusting of snow, the Longbourn party walked the short distance. Mr Pierce gave a rousing sermon about the miracle of the birth of the Christ child, followed by the concluding prayers. After a concluding hymn, the service was over.

The Bingley, Pierce, and Phillips families joined the party at Longbourn for the massive feast served for Christmas dinner. As was the norm at Longbourn, there was no precedence observed and everyone sat with whomever they wished.

Elizabeth was thankful that Will seemed to be back to normal and there was none of the distance she had felt on the journey into town. When she had mentioned his behaviour to her mother, she had reminded her daughter of William's behaviour all those years ago that had nothing to do with his feelings for her, rather it was *because* of his feelings. She reminded her daughter that if he had feelings now, he would have to wait until she was out, so it was very likely his way of trying to regulate himself.

When she really considered her mother's words, Elizabeth had seen the truth of them, so rather than take offence, she showed understanding. As they sat across the table from each other, she caught him staring at her he was wont to do, and rather than look away, they held each other's eyes and she gave him a wide and warm smile. It was the first time that each truly began to understand that mayhap the other reciprocated their feelings.

The day after Christmas, Elizabeth was summoned to see her brother and mother to discuss the Twelfth Night ball the Bennets were holding. After consulting with Tammy and Thomas Bennet, they discovered that unlike those that were held in town, there would be no inappropriate behaviour or suggestive games played at the Bennets' party; it would essentially just be a normal ball that happened to be held on Twelfth Night. Due to this, Elizabeth was informed by Andrew and her mother that she would be allowed to dance at the ball, though only with family or close friends that were approved ahead of time by Andrew. Luckily there were more than enough family.

When Will found out that Elizabeth would be permitted to dance at the ball, he lit up, but the light was dimmed as Andrew mentioned that his sister would not dance more than once with *any* man that night. Will found Elizabeth sitting in her birth father's library and petitioned her for the supper set, which she granted with pleasure.

Elizabeth thought that her brother's one set rule was high-handed, but no amount of cajoling caused him to relent. Richard would dance the first, followed by father Bennet, and then Andrew, Ian Ashby, and then William Bennet would have the set before the supper set. John Manning would dance with her the set after the meal, Perry, then Uncles George, Edward, and Frank would fill out the rest of her dance card. Andrew was relieved that Lizzy's card was filled by family only.

~~~~~~~~/~~~~~~~~

The night of the ball, Elizabeth felt the thrill of excitement which can only come when something is unknown. The only other place she had danced was in one of the family's houses with a dancing master. She had danced with her Fitzwilliam brothers, Perry, and William before, but she had never been to a ball before and was grateful that, in Meryton, girls were allowed to attend local events from the age of sixteen.

She had to admit that as much as she was happy to be dancing for each set, if she had only been allowed to dance the supper set with Will, it would have been enough. Not only would she dance with him, but he would be her partner at supper!

The ball room was lit with what looked like a thousand candles so that it was practically as light as day inside. There were chairs lining the walls with a long table for punch bowls and other refreshing drinks on one side.

Richard led his sister to the floor for the first set and she revelled in the experience. Then all was a blur until Will came to collect her for the supper set. She rested her hand on his arm lightly, but she was very aware of his body heat through his sleeve and her glove.

Will was as much in anticipation for their dance as his partner was. He had danced every set so far, not wanting to leave anyone without a partner if she desired to dance. He had thrown his 1797 calendar away with glee and now he had started crossing off days in 1798. Just over a year before he could start courting her unofficially!

The dance was magical for them both, and when they were separated by the line, they each felt bereft of the other's company. At the end of the set, Will led Elizabeth to a table with other family members and went to fill her plate for her.

None of the parents sitting two tables over missed the dreamy look on Elizabeth's face or the besotted look on Will's. Lady Anne was thinking how much she would love to have Lizzy as a daughter while Lady Elaine was thinking about how close
~~~~~~~~

her daughter would live to Snowhaven if things progressed, once she was out. At the same table as the aforementioned couple, Andrew and Richard both suspected that Will would become their brother...one day sooner rather than later!

January 10, 1798

The Darcys and the Fitzwilliams arrived at their respective estates around midday on the tenth day of January. Branch made his walk to the kitchens, then was led to the master's study. The master confirmed that the date for the note that would be put in the knothole had not changed. As Jones returned to his shared room with Branch, he overheard the head coachman and the butler talking about how the two families would meet at Pemberley on the second day of April then travel to some house in the Lake District, and that there would only be two outriders per family coach.

Jones knew that this was exactly what his employer wanted, so he said that this message he would deliver to the hiding place himself. He did, and of course, within minutes of him departing Kympton, Branch had replaced Jones' note in the hole with his.

~~~~~~~~/~~~~~~~~

Just like Jones had said to do before the detour to London, when her footman checked the place where notes were left seven days after Twelfth Night the missive was waiting for him. He pushed his mount as hard as he could to get the note to his mistress as he knew that this was more than likely the note that she was wanting above all others.

He vaulted off his horse at Mrs Fitzpatrick's house before the animal had made a complete stop, pushed his way past the housekeeper, and placed the note into his mistress' hands as if it were the most precious thing in the world. She gave him a dismissive wave as she told him to close the door to make sure that she was not disturbed until she rang her bell.

She opened the note and read:

Both families leave Pem. 2 April to Lakes by route described previously. 2 outriders per family coach.
~~~~~~~~

If she had been one of her low-class servants, Mrs Fitzpatrick would have jumped for joy. Her victory was almost at hand! A scant three months, no more than that, and she would watch them die, all of them, especially the foundling. She knew that Wickham would like to be the one to kill the so-called 'Lady Elizabeth' and she might even allow him to have his sport with her.

She wrote a note for McLamb and rang her bell. "Take this to McLamb," she instructed her footman and waved him away. She felt as close to euphoric as she had in many a year. She then wrote another note that she would have the footman place in the knothole on the morrow.

~~~~~~~~/~~~~~~~~

Two days later, the guard keeping watch on the tree saw a man open the cover and place a note inside. He retrieved it once he was certain that the rider had left, and had a boy run it to Branch at Pemberley. Branch took the note to the master who read it.

Lay low, leave on the second of April after the fools depart Pemberley, when you get to me, I will gladly pay you the balance I owe you for your work.

Mrs F.

Mrs F. meant nothing to George Darcy, but after she had written so many vitriol- laced letters to Pemberley, he was sure that he recognised the writing. He asked Douglas to request that his wife join him in the study. When Anne entered, he handed her the note.

"Catherine!" was the only word she uttered, which confirmed what he knew.

After his wife departed, the master turned to Branch. "Wait a few days and then tell Jones you checked the hole and found this." He handed the note to the faithful guard who placed it in his pocket.
~~~~~~~~

CHAPTER 17

April 1798

Richard had requested and was granted leave from the end of March. He was sorry to have missed Lizzy's seventeenth birthday, but he had been required to choose what days he most wanted off, and being there when they confronted the villains was imperative. He would be part of the group traveling; of that there was no question. Still, he could not believe that she was already so grown. In less than a year his baby sister would come out into society. As much as he would have liked to be present at Georgie's and her joint celebration, it was much more important that he be here now. And as hard as it was to grasp his sister's age, it was just as hard to think that their 'little' Georgie had just turned fourteen.

The well of love and the need to protect them turned his thoughts to the upcoming confrontation. They were now certain Lady Catherine de Bourgh was involved, and Richard was hoping that Wickham was somehow connected to the insane lady and would be present when the criminals were apprehended. He dearly hoped that the murderer would give him the slightest provocation, as he had a debt to repay after the miscreant had tried to murder his little sister.

The Bennets were at Snowhaven, having arrived some days before the celebration of Elizabeth's birthday. Bennet had used any excuse that he could conjure to call at Pemberley and lose himself among the shelves of his friend's library, but his true reason for being present was to offer whatever support he could in the upcoming endeavour.

On the final day of March, the men met in Andrew's study

to go over their plans again, to make sure that they had taken every possible contingency into account. Richard confirmed that a group of ex-soldiers who were experienced in the art of camouflage had been hidden in the woods around the suspected ambush site for more than a sennight and had since reported that four men had scouted the area in question. More men had returned the day before and cut down two trees, placing them on either side of the carriage trail to be moved into place on the day of the attack.

Branch reported that Jones was still oblivious to the fact that he had been under observation, and Forester confirmed that his men were ready. He would command a combined force of both Pemberley's and Snowhaven's guards of close to fifty men not counting additional ex-soldiers that Richard had hired. But as the criminals had been led to expect, there would only be two outriders beside each coach.

Elizabeth wished that she could be more involved in the development and execution of the plan, but she accepted that the men would not allow any women or children in the vicinity of the ambush area. She sat in an armchair in her sitting room with Aggie's head in her lap as she scratched her behind her ears. She listened to pleasurable grunts from her dog as her tail thumped the carpet. Each time Elizabeth would stop her ministrations, Aggie would put her head under one of her mistress' hands, indicating her desire for more petting.

Elizabeth considered the significance of her being seventeen. In ten months, ten short months, she would come out, and she was hoping, becoming more and more certain, that Will would ask for the two significant sets after the first which she would dance with Andrew and then Richard. She was as sure as she had ever been about anything in her feelings for Will, he was the only one that she would ever agree to marry. Wes had thankfully reduced his attentions, she surmised after reading the obvious signs that her affections were not engaged by him.

After the participants of the meeting had dispersed, Will had taken a ride on Jupiter to expend some pent-up energy.

His thoughts were firmly directed to his exquisite cousin Elizabeth. When he was not busy with some occupation, and even sometimes when he was, she completely inhabited his thoughts. There was nothing he could or desired to do to evict her from being so, for she was as beautiful inside as she was outside, and he could imagine naught but a lifetime of her challenging him and correcting him in long debates.

He could also see them on a sable throw in front of a roaring fire not wearing anything... He stopped himself before the oft-repeated fantasy again went too far and this would not be enough. Less than ten months' worth of days to cross off and she would be out. Even though he knew that Andrew would not allow him to request an official courtship for some months after, he was determined that she would have no doubt of his intentions. If the looks and smiles she gave him were any indication, his affections were returned in full measure, and thinking about that made his heart race.

~~~~~~~~/~~~~~~~~

Jones was already imagining what he would be spending his money on. He was also planning how he would disappear once he received his reward from Mrs Fitzpatrick— before he paid the promised amount to Branch. Why should he share his hard-earned bounty?

He would follow the instructions and depart once the carriages left Pemberley on the second. Branch would be assisting one of the coachmen, so it was possible that, depending on her plan, he may not have to worry about Branch after the morrow anyway.

Jones was right about one thing, Branch would be with the carriages, not on one, but with an additional twenty men inside them, not the woman and children that were expected. He gave strict instructions that as soon as the convoy was no longer visible from the stables that Jones be taken into custody. He had no doubt that had he truly been working with him; Jones would have double-crossed him.

He was confident that the master and the Lieutenant-Col-
~~~~~~~~

onel's plan was sound. There was always a chance of things not going according to plan in the heat of battle, but it was also true that every possible contingency had been covered. If Branch had still been in the army, the younger Fitzwilliam brother was the kind of officer that he would have followed anywhere.

~~~~~~~~/~~~~~~~~

Mrs Fitzpatrick was supremely confident; her plan would work because it was, after all, her plan, and she was never wrong. Her carriage would transport her close to the site of her triumph so she would watch it happen. With her two footmen having set up a table and chair for her on a slight rise, she would be able to view the culmination of all these years of waiting, to watch her former family finally receive their comeuppance.

It renewed her anger at Hodges for killing her former brother, as she truly would have wanted that privilege for herself. As it was, she planned to watch Wickham strangle the life out of the foundling the man had called his daughter.

Wickham could not believe that the day was here and that his vengeance was finally at hand. They were at an inn in a town just a few hours from the sight of the ambush. Disguised in a wig and with his hat pulled as far down as possible, Wickham had worked closely with McLamb to scout the area and confirmed that their employer was correct, that the place she chose would have to be traversed by a party travelling from Pemberley to the Lake District.

He remembered the conversation a fortnight earlier when the old bat had finally revealed her plan to him.

"You summoned me, madam," Wickham stated dryly.

"Do not be impertinent, boy," she said as she lifted her cane, reminding him that he needed to be careful how he spoke to her.

"Sorry, Mrs Fitzpatrick," he replied using as much fake contrition as he could muster.

"In a fortnight, all of those who have wronged us will be dead," she relayed in a tone that conveyed this as a matter of fact. She had gone on to tell him the when and where. "You will help scout the area with McLamb due to your superior knowledge of the terrain around
~~~~~~~~

Pemberley." He had nodded, never pointing out that it had in fact been many years since he had been anywhere near the environs of Pemberley. "As long as you perform well, you will be rewarded, and I may even start paying you for your work."

"May I make a request in lieu of any other reward," he ventured. She inclined her head like the Queen would indicate he should continue. "I would like to kill the foundling myself, and I ask for Miss Darcy to use and then I will dispose of her after," he asked, hoping that she would fall for his ploy regarding Miss Darcy.

"The foundling is yours, but Miss Darcy must die with the rest of them. I want none of them alive with any claim on my soon to be properties," she told him with finality.

"Thank you for the foundling," he bowed and then left her company as she had given him a dismissive wave.

Worrying that McLamb would report to the old bat, he rethought the plan to involve him in his attempt to take Miss Darcy for himself. Wickham knew that in the midst of it all, he would have to find a way to fool the old bat, to make her think that Georgiana was dead. He then would take her, once the action had subsided with him "dead" as well. Mayhap she would be so grateful for saving her life that she would willingly give herself to him.

~~~~~~~/~~~~~~~

As planned, three carriages arrived from Snowhaven on the first day of April. As Jones watched them arrive, his excitement built because he knew that he would soon be able to stop pretending to be a stable hand. On the morrow, he would be rid of the hated tasks forever. If he never had to muck out a stall in his life again, it would be too soon for him.

The family congregated in the largest drawing room after the arrivals changed. The part that they would play in the illusion on the morrow was again discussed. They did not think that they were being watched, but they would take no chances, just in case there was a watcher that had been missed.

The ladies were not overjoyed that their menfolk would be in the vicinity of the action but were assured that the only one
~~~~~~~

who would be close at the point of contact would be Richard. He needed to be able to survey the field of the confrontation for any unexpected problems that would necessitate changes in strategy. Although they had to plan for it, knowing how their adversary needed to feel that she controlled everything, there was little chance of there being a deviation from the plan she had most certainly laid out.

To keep the impression that all was normal, a group of the younger family members took a ride that afternoon, though the usual banter that one would expect from the family members was subdued. Elizabeth steered Saturn over towards Zeus until she was riding parallel to her cousin with Aggie trotting in between them. "Please do not get hurt on the morrow," Elizabeth begged softly. "I do not want to imagine not having you to...talk to." Elizabeth realised how close she had come to declaring her feelings. But even without hearing the words, Will understood her meaning.

"As I cannot imagine the same about you, Lizzy. We will all be well, I promise," he replied tenderly.

"That is a promise I will hold you to," she replied with a half-smile, both fully aware of the double meaning of her statement and that they had just declared their intentions without having to wait. After all the anxiety, it was so simply done. With a clarity that often comes when one is facing an unknown, they smiled ruefully as each wondered how it had gotten so far astray when they were both so very good at using their words and reading between the lines. They stayed close to one another but rode on without more discussion. No more really needed to be said.

That evening there was a quiet dinner as everyone contemplated the significance of the next day. Andrew and George were pleased that Bennet would remain at Pemberley with the women and children so they would not be bereft of all the men in the family, and he faithfully promised to let their women work themselves into a frenzy.

~~~~~~~/~~~~~~~

Forester and his fifty men had been at Snowhaven for a sen-
~~~~~~~

night and were ready to finish this. This way if anyone was sent to verify the family's departure, they would not see a suspicious mass exodus of horsemen following the supposedly unaccompanied carriages.

As there was a full moon, a little after one in the morning, Forester led his men toward their waiting points by a circuitous route. Before five they were in place and well back from the spots where they knew the criminals would be.

~~~~~~~~/~~~~~~~~

McLamb led his group of mercenaries out of the inn as the dawn broke. Wickham rode next to him and the riders were followed by Mrs Fitzpatrick in her carriage with her two footmen in their positions on the bench behind the compartment.

Wickham could taste the victory and was already spending the money that would be his in a matter of days. If there were more time, he would have dragged the foundling into the woods and ruined her to prove his power and superiority, but if he wanted to somehow make sure that Miss Darcy lived, he would have to kill her faster than he had intended to.

Mrs Fitzpatrick was sitting on the comfortable seat, leaning against the squabs with a self-satisfied smile on her lips. She would make them kneel before her, hear her grievances against them, hear them begging for their lives and the lives of their precious brats before she ordered them shot. Mayhap she would do some shooting herself. This was going to be the best day in her life since she had dispatched that useless husband of hers and found that will, which ruined all her plans.

For her, the icing on the cake was her belief that her insipid, sickly daughter and that Ashby who had married her would be part of the party so she would be able to rid the world of them, too. She felt so relaxed that she did something that she had not since she was a young girl—she dozed in the equipage.

~~~~~~~~/~~~~~~~~

The precautions had been worth taking because one of McLamb's men was indeed watching from afar, hidden in a spot that Wickham had told him about. He saw the convoy of carriages pull into the courtyard of the manor house and he counted six outriders standing ready next to their mounts in the drive. Until the carriages blocked his view, he saw what he believed were members of the family standing ready at the top of the stairs. Once his view was obscured by the equipages, he sat back and waited. His instruction was to ride like the wind as soon as the carriages started to move.

~~~~~~~~/~~~~~~~~

As planned, the women and children descended the stairs and then when completely hidden by the assembled coaches, they entered the servants' entrance under the stairs. Each of the five carriages contained four heavily armed guards. The drivers and footmen each had a brace of pistols at hand. Branch was sitting next to the driver of the second conveyance in the line. As the men would be expected to do, they mounted their horses to ride alongside the coaches.

~~~~~~~~/~~~~~~~~

McLamb's man watched as the carriages exited the courtyard and turned onto the drive. The outriders took up stations between the men riding alongside the coaches. The man, who thought that he had been unobserved, jumped onto his horse and took off at full gallop towards the waiting ambush.

The two men who had been watching him, waited until he left the estate by taking the road that the carriages would soon travel.

~~~~~~~~/~~~~~~~~

Jones leaned on his shovel as he watched the carriages disappear over the rise in the drive. He threw his shovel down with disgust and turned. There blocking his way, were three footmen. One of them was the huge beast that always accompanied Lady Elizabeth. But if Biggs was standing in front of him, then who was in the carriages?

He unwisely tried to turn and run, but before he could move, Biggs, with catlike reflexes, had knocked him to the ground with a blow that carried the force of a blacksmith's hammer.
~~~~~~~~

"Ya thought we were fooled by the likes of ya?" Biggs said as he grabbed Jones by the collar and lifted him to his feet as if he weighed nothing. He nodded to the two footmen next to him. One fastened irons on Jones's ankles and the other on his wrists.

Rather than being on his way to freedom, Jones found himself thrown none too gently into the windowless coal cellar.

~~~~~~~~/~~~~~~~~

His man rode in, and notified him that the victims were on their way, and a half hour or less behind him. McLamb ordered his men to pull the two trees into place and take up stations. Next, he instructed them to take up stations on either side of the carriage trail per his employer's exacting instructions.

When quizzed, the man confirmed that they were carrying many trunks. McLamb was looking forward to picking over the personal jewellery and the other items that were packed after the riders were executed. Being able to take anything they desired, including well over thirty horses, had made this job all the more attractive, even making putting up with 'her majesty' somewhat bearable.

Wickham felt the anticipation of the fast-approaching time when he would see those he hated die, one especially and directly by his hand. As he stood behind the tree, he felt to make sure that the pistol in his belt was firmly in place and ready to fire. He did not bother to wear his disguise; in his mind, there was no need.

Mrs Fitzpatrick was sitting at her table on the outcrop of rocks that allowed her to survey the scene of her impending victory in all her imperious glory, waiting for the moment that she had long dreamt of.

~~~~~~~~/~~~~~~~~

Richard had joined Forester ahead of the first of the carriages entering the ambush area. Along with the men who had been secreted in the woods beforehand, there were thirty men to each side of the trail some yards behind, where the miscreants were waiting. He identified his former aunt sitting at her table as if she were about to watch a cricket match. He accepted that she was insane, but neither insanity nor anything else would save her from justice this day.

He saw Wickham stick his head out from behind a tree opposite from the side that Richard and Forester were on. His first inclination was to charge forward and end the man, but he stayed as Will walked up behind him and rested a hand on his shoulder. "There will be time for that after," he told his most dangerous cousin.

As the attackers watched, the lead coach entered the clearing. As it took the bend, it was forced to halt due to trees across the trail which were blocking the way forward. The other coaches came to a halt, and the drivers and riders looked suitably confused.

At that moment McLamb and his men revealed themselves. "Stand and deliver!" A very confident McLamb called out as his men trained their weapons on the drivers and riders.

Mrs Fitzpatrick knew how it would be; her plan had been flawless!

The End of Book 3

COMING SOON:

June/July 2021 - yet untitled Bad Bennet Story

The working title is '*The Bad Brother*' but I am not certain that it will be the title by the time I complete the tale. In this book, that is a WIPWIP as Book 3 is published. James & Thomas Bennet are twins with James born first. The boys start out as best friends but as he gets older Thomas becomes to resent his brother more and more rather than looking at for the blessings in his own life.

When Thomas reached his majority, James Bennet Senior despairs what to do with he jealous and resentful son so unknown to the father has become a drunk and gamester. The father releases Thomas's legacy to him and all connection is lost until on the death of his parents, Thomas returns after gambling hi large legacy away expecting more money and is frustrated. He had his wife Fanny leave Longbourn threatening revenge.

At the point that we join the story, James and Pricilla Bennet of Longbourn have a happy and contented family comprising of Jamie, the oldest and his sisters Jane, Elizabeth and Mary. The selfish and grasping Thomas and Fanny Bennet have two daughters, of questionable parentage, Kitty and Lydia.

The Gardiners and Phillips are present but they are not related by blood or marriage to the main characters, or each other. The story concentrates on the Bennets and Darcys, but Wickham, Collins, the de Bourghs, and Fitzwilliams are also woven into the fabric of this tale.

August/September 2021
William Bennet Finds Love

A sequel to the Discarded Daughter Series

By the end of book 4 you will know who William Bennet (ex-William Collins) falls in love with and marries. It is a very unexpected paring to all of the characters as there had been a suspicion by the families on both sides that the lady in question would be courted by another Bennet brother.

The story will start when William Collins is already William Bennet and will concentrate on the most unlikely pairing. Other characters from the Discarded Daughter series will be woven into the story but the concentration will be on the friendship, courtship, betrothal, and eventual marriage of William Bennet and his lady love.

BOOKS IN THIS SERIES

https://kdp.amazon.com/en_US/series/R7NXNEPQTAQ

The Discarded Daughter series is a 4- book series. Book 2 and 3 are now complete and Book 4 in being edited.

This series looks at the life of Elizabeth Bennet who is kidnapped to be killed on the orders of her demented mother, Fanny. The story also looks at the characters in her life, both good and bad, and the effect that she has on them.

When she is found will she improve the life of her adoptive family? How will she be accepted by their wider family? We also see the effects on those who have lost her. How do they cope with the loss? What of Fanny, will she get her just rewards? Will Thomas Bennet hide in his study or will he become the father that we all wish him to be?

The tale starts before Elizabeth's birth and the series will end at some point when Elizabeth is an adult. We will follow her life through the highs and lows, love and loss. If you are looking for a series that only concentrates on the main character then this will not be for you. This story is essentially about the love of family. There are cliff-hangers at the end of some of the books, but they are answered soon in the following book. There will be a short wait between publication of one book to the next so you will not be left with questions for too long. I hope that you enjoy my second series.

Book 1 – Discarded

This is Book 1 of a 4-book series.

In Book 1 we are introduced to the characters both the heroes and the villains. Elizabeth makes the grievous mistake of being born a girl when Fanny Bennet is convinced that she will be a son. After first accusing the midwife of substituting her son for a daughter, Fanny rejects her daughter and accuses her of being a demon sent from the devil.

This tale is not just about Elizabeth but about the characters in her life, both good and bad, and the effect that she has on them. We also see the effects on those who have lost her.

Thomas Bennet does everything that he can to protect his second daughter but Fanny finds a way to have Elizabeth kidnapped and she demands that the man kill her daughter and deliver proof when the deed is done.

Fanny's insanity driven actions lead to Elizabeth being discarded far from home. Will she be found? If so by whom? How will her life unfold? What of the Bennets and especially the evil Fanny?

Book 1 follows Elizabeth's life from birth until she is about seven or eight years old. Yes, there is a cliff-hanger at the end of Book 1, but we get the answers within the first chapter or two of Book 2.

Book 2 – Recovery

This is Book 2 of a 4-book series.

We left Lizzy lying prostrate under her beloved cob Astraea. Her father falls to his knees in tears, after losing Tiffany will the Earl and Countess of Matlock be able to overcome this tragedy if they lose their daughter? As we can all surmise, Lizzy has to survive for the story to continue, so what will her physical impediments, if any, be?

Book 2 covers another eight years of Elizabeth's life and the lives of her family, and the family that she was stolen from. Is Martha and Louisa Bingley's reformation real and what of Miss Caroline at the Dark Hollow School? Will it improve her or will she just become more determined to get her own way?

We find out what happens to George Wickham and his life with the ex-Lady Catherine de Bourgh, now Mrs. Fitzpatrick. What are her plans for him and to extract revenge for the perceived ills that have been perpetrated against her? This book also ends with a cliff-hanger that is answered in the first few lines of Book 3.

BOOKS BY THIS AUTHOR

A Change Of Fortunes

What if, unlike canon, the Bennets had sons? Could it be, if both father and mother prayed to God and begged for a son that their prayers would be answered? If the prayers were granted how would the parents be different and what kind of life would the family have? What will the consequences of their decisions be?

In many Pride and Prejudice variations the Bennet parents are portrayed as borderline neglectful with Mr. Bennet caring only about making fun of others, reading and drinking his port while shutting himself away in his study. Mrs. Bennet is often shown as flighty, unintelligent and a character to make sport of. The Bennet parent's marriage is often shown as a mistake where there is no love; could there be love there that has been stifled due to circumstances?

In this book, some of those traits are present, but we see what a different set of circumstances and decisions do to the parents and the family as a whole. Most of the characters from canon are here along with some new characters to help broaden the story. The normal villains are present with one added who is not normally a villain per se and I trust that you, my dear reader, will like the way that they are all 'rewarded' in my story.

We find a much stronger and more resolute Bingley. Jane Bennet is serene, but not without a steely resolve. I feel that both need to be portrayed with more strength of character for the purposes of this book. Sit back, relax and enjoy and my hope is that you will be suitably entertained.

The Hypocrite

The Hypocrite is a low angst, sweet and clean tale about the relationship dynamics between Fitzwilliam Darcy and Elizabeth Bennet after his disastrous and insult laden proposal at Hunsford. How does our heroine react to his proposal and the behaviour that she has witnessed from Darcy up to that point in the story?

The traditional villains from Pride and Prejudice that we all love to hate make an appearance in my story BUT they are not the focus. Other than Miss Bingley, whose character provides the small amount of angst in this tale, they play a very small role and are dealt with quickly. If dear reader you are looking for an angst filled tale rife with dastardly attempts to disrupt ODC then I am sorry to say, you will not find that in my book.

This story is about the consequences of the decisions made by the characters portrayed within. Along with Darcy and Elizabeth, we examine the trajectory of the supporting character's lives around them. How are they affected by decisions taken by ODC coupled with the decisions that they make themselves? How do the decisions taken by members of the Bingley/Hurst family affect them and their lives?

The Bennets are assumed to be extremely wealthy for the purposes of my tale, the source of that wealth is explained during the telling of this story. The wealth, like so much in this story is a consequence of decisions made Thomas Bennet and Edward Gardiner.

If you like a sweet and clean, low angst story, then dear reader, sit back, pour yourself a glass of your favourite drink and read, because this book is for you.

The Duke's Daughter: Omnibus Edition

All three parts of the series are available individually.

Part 1: Lady Elizbeth Bennet is the Daughter of Lord Thomas and Lady Sarah Bennet, the Duke and Duchess of Hertfordshire. She is quick to judge and anger and very slow to forgive. Fitzwilliam Darcy has learnt to rely on his own judgement above all others. Once he believes that something is a certain way, he does not allow anyone to change his mind. He ignored his mother and the result was the Ramsgate debacle, but he had not learnt his lesson yet.
He mistakes information that her heard from his Aunt about her parson's relatives and with assumptions and his failure to listen to his friends the Bingleys, he makes a huge mistake and faces a very angry Lady Elizabeth Bennet.

Part 2: At the end of Part 1, William Darcy saved Lady Elizabeth Bennet's life, but at what cost? After a short look into the future, part 2 picks up from the point that Part 1 ended. We find out very soon what William's fate is. We also follow the villains as they plot their revenge and try to find new ways to get money that they do not deserve.
Elizabeth finally admitted that she loved William the morning that he was shot, is it too late or will love find a way? As there always are in life, there are highs and lows and this second part of three gives us a window into the ups and downs that affect our couple and their extended family.

Part 3: In part 2, the Duke's Daughter became a Duchess. We follow ODC as they continue their married life as they deal with the vagaries of life. We left the villains preparing to sail from Bundoran to execute their dastardly plan. We find out if they are successful or if they fail.

In this final part of the Duke's Daughter series, we get a good idea what the future holds for the characters that we have followed through the first two books in the series.

Made in United States
Orlando, FL
15 May 2024

46894669R00114